Kindle

epub

Shadow Man

Shadow Man

By

Vicki M Taylor

"Black eyes and blue tears" published in WOW anthology © 2008

"Indian Giver" published in Darker Times Anthology Volume Six © 2014

My Griefs: Passing on, previously published in "Journey's End: Death, Dying, and the End of Life by Victoria Brewster and Julie Saeger Nierenberg © 2017

An Anthology of Pencil Me In "Out of the Box" © 2017 "The Magic Miracle",
"Indian Giver", "Lightning Response", "My Anxiety vs His Protection", "The North Elevator"

ISBN 978-0-9838586-6-9 (trade paperback)

Dedication

To Him. The man who helped me gain the strength to escape the shadow man, defeat the darkness and conquer the night terrors. My loving husband, Greg. The only man who loved me enough to discover who I was and helped me discover "me" as well. He is and will always be the love of my life.

Other Books by Author, Vicki M. Taylor

- Forever Until We Meet
- Not Without Anna
- Trust in the Wind
- March Madness - novella
- Catch of the Season - novella
- Second Glances Second Chances - novella
- Out For Justice

Table Of Contents

Shadow Man

PTSD and ME

Hello, Readers,

The triggers start now. The sexual abuse started when I was five years old and lasted until I was thirteen. The physical abuse started when I was two years old. It was at that time I learned that I had angels watching over me and I knew about my God who took away all my hurts and pains. God took away all my memories and replaced them with darkness. A deep darkness so far into itself that I could never find my way out.

Even now, to this day, that darkness still exists. And If I'm not careful, I might fall into it.

I wrote short stories as a way of putting distance between me and the world. Me and others. Me and myself.

I'm not a stranger to silence. It's been with me all my life. I disappear into the darkness and the silence envelopes me. I can get lost in the silence. I can be me in the silence. No one else knows me in the silence. The Shadow Man had a way of following me. He and others found me in the Marine Corps and repeatedly raped me. I dove deep into the darkness afterwards. No one can find me in the silence.

It hurts my head and makes me want to cry to think of why I needed the darkness. My breathing gets fast. I know there are reasons. I don't care to know what they are. My imagination and ideas are enough. I don't know the real thing. I don't want to know the real thing. I've been in therapy for over 25 years. I've never dealt with past regression. God is protecting me from that for a reason. I don't need to go messing around and screw around with my head, memories and regression therapy. It's not going to be helpful. I have already forgiven everyone. I had to… it was God who told me to. I follow Christ and forgiveness comes from Christ. It doesn't mean that it makes everything all right and everything is going to be okay. Shit still happened. Stuff a five-year-old should never have had to deal with. Let alone have a 13-year-old stand at the foot of her adopted father's bed after extricating herself from his hands between her legs from sleeping and tell him he will never touch her again. Never. Ever.

Without God, I would not be here today. That is all His doing. And I know that in another life, God would do that same thing all over again. That's the story He's written for me. And I'm following His journey set forth for me. It's His path I'm walking. With Him by my side. With Him walking with me, I'm not afraid. If it gets dark again, I know there's going to be a good reason why. And God will be there to help me through it.

I end this compilation of short stories with a gift to God. A poem I wrote to Him. I believe In Him. I know that He believes in me. He told me so. I believe Him.

This short story compilation is a revelation. I write from dark to light. I follow the path of my life, from dark to light. I hope that you find the message, too.

All my best and for those needing to escape their shadow man, there is hope.

Vicki.

Silence

Such a fickle creature -- my friend, my foe.
I welcome my friend with open arms when my
senses overload.
You envelop me in your blanket of stillness,
comforting me.
My protector. My safe harbor.

I control your absence of sound, for me, you are my
slave.
And I, I am the master.
Mean-spirited you are, my foe, dark silence.

I quiver at your abrupt entry, startling my senses.

You swoop down, blanking all thought, all
consciousness, frightening me.
My fears magnify. My terrors grow.
You control my imagination; I am your unwilling
servant.

And you, you are my captor
Silence, are you my friend or foe?

The Shadow Man

I don't sleep.

The shadow man comes if I close my eyes.

I stay awake.

It's so hard. I'm so little.

I must stay awake. Awake a long time after everyone in the house falls asleep. The animals are quiet outside. No dogs bark. No birds sing.

My eyes want to close.

No! The shadow man will come.

Don't go to sleep. Sing your ABCs. Not too loud, don't let anyone hear.

It's getting later. I forget my ABCs. I can't help it. My eyes close. Just for a few minutes. Maybe more. Wake up!

Don't sleep!

My heart pounds in my small chest. I'm breathing very fast. Does the shadow man know I fell asleep. Is he coming?

Don't sleep!

I'm a big girl. I can stay awake. I'm going to be six years old.

I'm awake. Too afraid to fall asleep.

A...B.....C........D.............E....................
.........F .... my eyes flash open.

The sun is shining

I tell myself I tried. I swipe at the tears that fall.
I'm a bad girl. I fell asleep.

The shadow man came.

###

The shadow man is always there. In the corner of my bedroom. He doesn't speak; not yet. He just waits.

I know why he waits. He waits for me to sleep.

He thinks I'm falling asleep.

I don't sleep.

I never sleep.

I can't sleep. Not long. Never enough.

My eyes watch him. Waiting.

I toss and turn.

I'm awake.

He knows.

I'm not going to sleep.

Not this time.

The shadow man moves.

I freeze. My eyes track him.

He moves again. Away from the corner.

It's late. Very late. Maybe even tomorrow already.

The shadow man moves silently closer.
He leans down. His lips touch my forehead. "Go to sleep." He leaves, closing the door behind him.

I lay there, then vigorously wipe his mark from my face.

Is it safe to sleep?

I look at the window. It's still dark. It would be okay to sleep now. Just a little while.

I don't know how to sleep. I try my ABCs again.

I hold up my hands, I can barely see them. Soon it will be lighter. I don't sleep. Not yet.

###

I don't sleep.

I never sleep.

Even after I escaped the shadow man, the nightmares stay.

If I don't sleep, I won't have them.

I sleep very little. Never enough. Neer at night.

Am I safe? The question is always there. Will I ever be safe?

I grow older. The questions never change.

I don't sleep.

The shadow man can't find me, but he exists in my terror-filled nights.

Days and night drift by.

I pray for the nights to go quickly. I pray for the
night terrors to leave me alone.

Stay awake or face a night terror. I don't sleep.
I need to protect myself from the night terrors.

The older I get the more options I must face the
terrors.

Reading and writing all night are replaced with

drinking and dancing. Drinking puts me to sleep. It

doesn't make the night terrors disappear.

I need something more. Drugs. I don't
question them. Can I sleep? I take whatever
I'm given. I don't know what they are. I don't
sleep. I'm awake for days.

Wrong drugs Wrong people. The shadow man
comes again in different forms. I'm afraid. I haven't
escaped. There are more!

The sleep never comes. I can't let it. I'm too afraid
of the night terrors. I'm too afraid of the shadow
man.

More drinking; more drugs. I need relief. I need total blankness.

It doesn't come. Why? Why won't the terrors leave me alone?

Is it only me? Am I the only one who suffers though this? I can't talk about it. No one knows.

How do I explain the shadow man and the night terrors. No one could ever understand.

The years go by.

Babies come. No sleep is a relief. I have an excuse. Waiting for and watching children is a 24-hour duty. I don't sleep. It's normal now. I'm like others.

Kids grow and leave home. Again, I have no excuse to stay awake.

God was always there protecting me. No matter the danger. He kept me safe.

Life happens. Families break apart. Shadow man comes and goes, still night terrors torture me.

God keeps me safe.

Coffee becomes my crutch It helps keep me awake. I fear sleep. More alcohol. Brings blanks. Terrible experiences. Dangerous blanks. Life threatening blanks.

###

Then he comes into my life.

He brings a sense of balance and peace.

For the first time I sleep. His presence builds a protective barrier around me and him. We become one.

I tentatively tell him my story.

He helps me seek help. Old habits are hard to break but can be done. Good habits can be formed. Doctors provide medication that helps me sleep … The night terrors continue. We keep searching for solutions.

He is always there for me. He holds me. Protects me. Let's me cry. Let's me stay awake and write. The writing helps.

Books are written. Dark thrillers. Alternate realities. Murder. Suicide. The characters in my mind all talk, wanting their stories written.

I even dream stories. The story ideas continue to flow.

We find the best psychiatrist after a move to accommodate his flying desires.

My night terrors are finally gone. I sleep.

With proper medication I am safe. My doctor understands.

Therapy that lasts 25 plus years and continues. Forgiveness given. Forgotten, no. Therapy treatments keep thoughts on present. Practice mindfulness. Practice meditation. Peace.

I am a warrior.

I am a survivor.

The End

…and justice for all.

Absently, I pressed a button and nearly jumped when the soda fell to the bottom with a loud ***thunk.*** I looked around the small room. I couldn't stay here. The walls closed in. My heart pounding, I searched for an exit, my only conscious thought to escape as quickly as possible.

I found it. A small patio at the rear of the room. I made my way through the scattered tables, not glancing up until I was in front of the glass door. I pushed through and breathed deeply of the warm air of another Philadelphia summer.

Through my dark sunglasses I could see that the small patio only had one large round concrete table with three curved stone benches around it. One bench was already taken. The girl was small and young, looking all of eighteen. She glanced up as I turned to leave. With half a smile and a nod of her head, she said, "It's okay, I don't mind."

"Thanks." I carefully placed my can of soda on the table, then set my purse next to it. Checking for ants, I brushed a few stray leaves from the stone bench and sat.

Trying not to appear eager, I took out my cigarettes and lighter, fumbling as I did so. I didn't have to look up to know that she was watching me. My first inhale was long. I sucked the hot smoke deep into my lungs. Only after I had taken my first puff did I look up. Her shoulders were thin, hunched over her frail body. A haunted look about the eyes made me question my decision to sit.

Her voice was soft, yet hesitant. As if she wasn't sure where to start, but knew she wanted to say something. "Are you here for the trial?"

The trial? As if there were any other? "Yeah," I said, "I'm here for the trial."

"So am I." She brushed her fingers at the bits of sand on the tabletop, then looked sideways at me through strands of long blonde hair. She didn't push them out of her face, just let them hang.

Self-conscious, I patted the scarf that covered my hair. Yes, it was still in place. My armor against recognition. "Can you tell me about it?" she asked, staring at my wrists.

"Hmmm?" Oh, shit. I knew the sleeves of my blouse weren't long enough, yet I wore it anyway. I looked down at the part of my arm she was staring at. The scars glared white and angry in the sunlight. Even after six months, they still looked scary, even to me.

I put my hands back down and pulled at the sleeves, trying to make them cover my hands. "No."

"Oh, I'm prying. I'm sorry." I breathed a sigh of relief.

We sat in silence. Then her childish inquisitiveness overrode her attempt at maturity. "Why not?"

I couldn't believe she asked me that. I looked up to see honest sympathy staring back at me from vaguely familiar blue eyes. Something inside of me made me change my mind. I'm not exactly certain of the reason, since I had already told this story so many times before. I started speaking, slowly at first, not sure how much to tell this stranger I had just met.

"It was six months ago. I had just gotten home from work." I hurried to explain that it was late when I had gotten home. "I worked as a cashier on the third shift at the local Safeway."

My table companion only nodded her head for me to continue. She kept blessedly quiet.

"Just as I opened my front door, I was hit from behind. I didn't know what it was at first. I didn't know anything until I heard the heavy breathing and felt the tight grip."

"Oh, my God! I would have freaked. Were you scared?"

"Terrified. I didn't scream at first, but when I did, he smacked me hard on the side of the head. I thought I was going to be knocked out, but I didn't faint." I lit another cigarette and stared at the glowing tip. I didn't say anything yet, and she kept silent.

It must have been difficult for her to stay quiet. But she did. That was good. I didn't think I could tell this any other way. I watched her face as I continued my story

"The grocery bag I was carrying fell to the door and everything inside scattered. Cans and stuff rolled every which way. The eggs broke. When I saw the yellow yolks running along the floor, something inside of me snapped. I grabbed for anything I could use to fight back. The first thing I grabbed was the vase on the counter. I smashed it upside his head."

I noticed her only reaction was to smile faintly. I thought I saw a quick flash of satisfaction in her reaction, but then it was gone.

"He staggered back enough for me to get a better look. He was wearing black jeans, a black sweatshirt, and a black ski mask. I raced for the phone, but he beat me to it and shoved me aside. I fell. Hard. He fell on top of me. He took out a knife and pressed it against my side. I stopped struggling."

"Is that when he tied your wrists?"

I had to give her credit. She was trying to hold back her curiosity. I held out my hands. The sleeves slid up from my wrists.

"Yes, he cut the phone cord and tied my hands and feet." I gently touched the scars on my wrist. "The scars you see here are the same as the ones on my ankles."

She nodded as if she understood, then motioned for me to continue, for the first time unable to speak.

Without realizing, I had settled into my story. Giving her more details than I had ever told anyone before. What is it about talking to a stranger that makes a personal story easier to tell?

"After he tied me with the phone cord he wandered around the apartment, smashing things randomly. Then he came back. I couldn't understand why my husband didn't come out of the bedroom to find out what the noise was about. I was sure it would have woken him up."

My hands shook as I picked up my soda and swallowed deeply. The cold fizzy liquid felt good against my dry throat. I took another swallow, more to gather my thoughts than because I was thirsty. I steadied myself, then asked her, "Are you sure you want to hear this?"

"Yes, "she said. "Please—continue." She touched my hand briefly and then clasped her purse close to her chest. Embarrassed, she put her elbows on the table, folded her hands, and then sat her chin upon them. I took that as an indication she was ready to hear the rest of my story. I hoped so.

"He cut my uniform off with the knife. Each time he pushed the knife into my clothes he would pierce my skin. I could feel the sharp point of the knife enter my body, and then he'd pull it back out. I screamed from the pain, but each time I did he slapped my face. Finally, he gagged me. I guess he didn't want to draw a lot of attention with my screaming. Each time blood stained my shirt, he'd make this strange laughing noise."

I closed my eyes, no longer sitting on the cold stone bench reciting my story once again to a stranger, but on the floor of my apartment watching as my lifeblood flowed from my body.

"With each cut, the knife went deeper, the cuts larger. I was lying in a pool of my own blood. I could see it everywhere. It was sticky. So thick. So warm. I was getting so cold. I think I passed out for a few minutes. He must have thought I was dead or close to it. I remember vaguely thinking that he must have killed my husband and had been waiting to ambush me. I know I wasn't thinking very clearly. Or seeing clearly. Everything had a reddish haze to it, like I was swimming in blood."

I opened my eyes to see how she would react to this gruesome recollection. She too, had her eyes closed. We sat in silence. She opened her eyes and said, "I'm so sorry. Did you ever see the attacker?"

"Yeah." I grimaced, shifting on the hard bench. "I lay motionless on the floor; he must have assumed I was dead. I watched his feet as they moved from the living room into the bedroom and back. When he came back, he was wearing different shoes. I noticed them right away. They were the ones I bought my husband about a week before -- you know, Topsides. He wasn't wearing the ski mask or

the black jeans anymore, either. He was
wearing khakis.

I drew a shallow breath, still remembering the
heavy smell of copper that had surrounded me
on the floor. I coughed. "My gag tasted like blood.
I kept my eyes as closed as I could and still see
what he was doing. He knelt, away from the
blood, and pushed at me. Only God knows how I
kept from screaming out from the pain. I wanted
him to think I was dead. If he thought
I was dead, maybe he'd leave. I prayed to God
that he would just leave."

I stopped to light another cigarette, then continued.
My hands no longer shook as I lit the tip of my
cigarette. "Hmmf." I grunted then smiled.

"What?" The girl blinked several times as if
awakening from a sleep.

"Oh—nothing. I was just thinking that if he hadn't
forgotten his cigarettes, I never would have seen
his face."

"So? What happened?"

"From where I was lying on the floor, I had a good
view of the front door."

"The door?"

22

"Yeah. All I saw was his back as he opened it to leave. Then, he stopped and turned around."

"What did he do?"

"He grabbed the pack of cigarettes on the counter. My husband's cigarettes. Then I saw his face—it was my husband's face."

I heard her sigh, then she whispered, "My father."
"What?" I wasn't sure I heard her right. "Your husband. He was my father."

"How? When?" It was my turn to ask questions. "He never said he'd been married before." Now I know why her blue eyes looked so familiar. Just one more secret he'd kept from me.

"Of course he wouldn't," she said as if choking on bitter bile. "Why would he tell his new wife that he killed his previous one?"

"Killed? Whoa!" My breath choked by a cold clamping vise. "Did the police know he did it?"

She asked me for a cigarette. While I handed it to her, I thought about this new revelation. How could my loving and caring husband of two years become this cold-blooded killer? What kind of monster had I gotten involved with? Why didn't I know?

After I lit her cigarette she said, "I don't know much. Only what my aunt—my mother's sister—told me. And the little I've uncovered on my own." She gripped her purse, her fingers digging into the imitation leather. "I was only two years old when it happened. It was in Colorado. My mother's sister took me in and raised me. He didn't want me. He refused to have any contact with me at all. He took all the insurance money and just left. It didn't matter to me. I hated him.

"You said he killed your mother. How?"

"I guess the same as he tried with you. He tied her up, cut her up, then left her for dead. He came back later, as if he had been out with his friends, and called the police. He acted the poor victim well, according to my aunt. Too well, for one detective; but they couldn't get any evidence to convict him"

incredulous, all I could do was stare at her. How could this be happening I stammered as I spoke, "when he came back - when I saw his face - he didn't look at me. He just grabbed his cigarettes and walked out the door." I slammed my fist on the table. "I prayed to God that I wouldn't die so I could tell the police who did this to me."

"Did he come back?"

Yeah, he came back. But it was too late. Apparently, a neighbor had heard my screams and called the police. It was about fifteen minutes before the police broke through the door."

"How did they get him?"

"I spent two weeks in intensive care before I was allowed to speak to the police. He acted like nothing happened. I pretended I didn't know while I was afraid he'd try to kill me again."

"That's when you told them?"

"Yeah."

"I guess he used the same story?"

"Looks that way. After I told the police what happened, they searched his locker at work and found the knife. I don't know why he kept it."

I slammed my empty soda can down on the table, unable to find the words to express my emotions. The girl jumped. I apologized, then asked her, "Why did you come today?"

"I had to."

"But why? What made you sit through that whole trial and listen to everyone's testimony, then ask me to tell you, my story?"

"I haven't been here the whole time. I just got in town today. My aunt kept in touch with the other detective from my mother's murder. He followed a few hunches when he heard about your case and put two and two together."

"So, you didn't really see the whole trial then?"

"No."

"So, why talk to me?"
"I really wanted to talk to you."

"But you could have done that from anywhere, any time. Why did you want to talk to me *now*?"

She shook her head, making her hair fly about her face and thin shoulders. She opened her mouth, but no words came out. "I needed to know--" She swallowed hard. "I don't really know. I had to see for myself. I had to see you."

I reached across and touched her hand.

"I don't remember my mother." She looked away, then looked back. "The detective said

26

you looked a little like her." She swiped at her face. "I needed to see for myself that he finally gets what he deserves."

I didn't know what to say. We sat for a few moments in silence.

We were both startled when the glass doors opened, and a man announced that the jury was back. We gathered our belongings and threw our empty soda cans into the trash. Silently, we walked back down the hall to the heavy double doors to the courtroom. A guard held one open for us to enter.

"Wait," I stopped her with a light touch on the arm. "What's your name?"

"Karen."

"Karen. Pretty name."

She half smiled.
"Is there anything I can do for you?"

She shook her head, a sad frown on her face. "Maybe you might let me write to you once in a while?"

I nodded my head as we walked back into the courtroom.

The entire crowd sat silent and expectant, watching the jury file back into their box and sit. Not one person on the jury would look anywhere except at the judge as he read from the jury's notes and then gave the paper back to the bailiff, who then handed it to the jury foreman.

"Mr. Foreman, has the jury reached a decision?"

The jury foreman stood. "Yes, Your Honor." He took the folded paper from the bailiff and held it in front of him.

"On the sole count of the indictment of attempted murder in the first degree, how does the jury find?"

The foreman cleared his throat, then said, "We find the defendant—guilty."

Gasps echoed in waves across the room. Then clapping started until it resounded in applause. The judge banged his gavel for silence.

I silently clasped my hands together in a prayer of thanks, then I looked over at the young girl. She only sat quietly. Oblivious to the joyous celebration around her, tears streamed down her face.

My heart went out to her.

Confusion ensued. I realized she would soon be an orphan. I stood, trying to push my way through the crowd to get to her.

###

She stood. I tried to catch her eye. She didn't look at me. She slipped past the other well-wishers, heading for the low rail that separated the crowd from the rest of the courtroom.
###

"Karen!" I called, but she didn't hear me.

An object appeared in her hand. She held her arm out. I thought she was going to give something to her father. A loud crack resounded through the room.

My foot ached. A large man plowed into me as he raced for the exit. Screams echoed in my ears. I lost sight of the small girl as several officers surrounded her and took the weapon from her limp hand.

"My God! Who is she?"

I turned to find the prosecuting attorney once again at my elbow. I stopped to answer his question.

""Someone who's going to need a good lawyer. Who would you recommend?"

The End

My Anxiety Vs. His Protection

"Thanks for cuddling," I whispered as he stretched, left my still warm body, and walked away without even a good-bye.

I watched him move within arm's distance and settle. He didn't glance at me.

I called his name only to watch him turned away.

So, that's how we played the game today.

I could hold out as long as he could.

Or so I thought. The clock ticked the minutes one by one. My anxiety worsened with each passing moment.

I called his name again. This time, adding a pleading note for good measure.

He lifted his head, measured my need, and returned to his daydreaming. I obviously wasn't in enough concern for his presence.

I attempted to read. I couldn't focus on the words. I turned on the television. The movie didn't capture my attention.

I threw the remote across the bed. Something in my gesture caught his attention. He left his position, joined me, and sat close. His head lay on my thigh. His breathing soft and measured.

I sank my hands in his soft white fur. I sighed with contentment. My anxiety soothed. I once again eased into the safety of his protection.

Jack, my American Eskimo dog, once again, spared me from an anxiety episode.

The End

Don't Ask, Don't Tell

I wasn't with my mother when she died; twelve other people were there. However, I doubt if my mother asked for them. You could call them twelve witnesses. Many of them were members of my father's family. The "victim's family" was how it was stated in the official newspaper report. The rest were made up of the press and a state attorney or two.

I wasn't allowed to attend my mother's execution. I guess I wasn't an "official" victim. I'm not even sure if I really wanted to be there. I'd only just found out about it a day or so before it took place.

Would the reality of being there changed the stark images I have in my mind?

Probably not.

Would I have wanted to see my father's family sitting smugly in the front row with small smiles of satisfaction on their faces as my mother drew her last breath?

Probably not.

Would it have made any difference to them if I were in the room?

Probably not.

According to the official report the entire ordeal went smoothly. The sedative was administered without incident. According to witnesses, my mother didn't even cry. They said she just closed her eyes and went to sleep. She probably didn't even know when the lethal doses of Pentothal, Pancuronium, and Potassium Chloride were injected.

I think that was for the best.

The day after the execution, I received a telephone call. "Miss Anderson?" the caller asked.
"Yes," I replied.

"Miss Charlotte Anderson?"

"Yes. Can I help you?"

"Sergeant Crawford from the State Correctional Facility. I, that is, we have a box from, well . . . um, from your mother, Miss Anderson."

I said nothing. I had no idea why the prison would call me now, after the execution.

"Miss Anderson?" Sgt. Crawford probably assumed I had hung up on him.

"Yes, I'm still here. Are you sure you have a box for me?"

"Yes, ma'am. Your mother left instructions that her stuff be given to you after her, uh, execution. I'm sorry if this is upsetting, but I have to follow orders."

"Don't worry, Sergeant, you're not upsetting me. I take it you'd like me to come and pick up the box?"

I agreed to be at the facility the next morning. During the drive I questioned my motives for even going to get the box. Why did I want it? It's not like I had kept in touch with my mother or my father before his death.

You could say I was the product of a bad environment. Or, you could say I was an accident waiting to happen. It doesn't matter now. They're both dead and out of my life forever.

Did it matter that murder was what took them away? Not entirely. Somewhere in the back of my mind, I must have known that one day one of them would kill the other. I'm glad I wasn't there to see it. I'd seen enough while I was there to last me a lifetime.

I ran away from home when I was fourteen. I'm not even sure my parents noticed I was gone.

If they did, they sure didn't act worried. No calls to the police. Not even a single "have you seen this girl?" poster. I was out of their life and apparently, they accepted it. I guess you could say I saved my own life twenty years ago. So, what in the hell was I doing by accepting a box from my dead mother?

The process for picking up the box was surprisingly simple. I thought I'd have to go through a lot of barred doors, endless corridors, and submit to a strip search. I was wrong. Secretly embarrassed, I reprimanded myself for letting my imagination go out of control. I scolded myself, then told myself no more watching those damn police shows on television. I was relieved I didn't have to succumb to a search of my body's various cavities.

The administrative office stood separate from the prison. If I hadn't seen the sign that indicated the property was a prison, I wouldn't have known the difference between it and any other office complex.

The officer in charge checked my identification then helped load the box into the trunk of my car. I was back on the road in under fifteen minutes.

During the ride home I purposely kept the radio loud and sung along with all the songs.

Anything to keep my mind off the box sitting in the trunk. I could almost feel weird vibes all the way up in the front seat. I mentally shook myself, then scolded myself for acting like the boogeyman was going to get me. It was just a box of stuff. That's all.

Why did an item or mention of the past start your mind hurtling down on all kinds of random tangents? My life was pretty darn good at the moment. I'd finally put my past behind. I'd gotten out of the business, and I had a nice nest egg to live on while I went to school. Even though I wasn't exactly sure what my major was, I felt damn proud of myself for completing my education, considering what I'd been through.

I know I was one of the lucky ones. I'd seen what the "life" had done to a lot of girls. Many never made it past their eighteenth birthday. Good thing I was considered "old" at twenty-four. I couldn't handle the unending flow of the nameless faces of smelly, drunken men who would paw at me for a few dollars. I'd worked hard. I'd kept out of the drugs and stayed away from the cops. Maggie even helped me get my GED so I could make something of myself.

I smiled at the thought of my old manager. Maggie Monroe, she called herself. To me, she was the closest thing to a mother I guess I'd ever have. Even if I did work for her. I remember when I told her I was leaving the business for good. She said, "Good for you, kid." Then she gave me this awkward hug and complained about mascara getting in her eyes making them water. I knew she was crying, but I'd never let on. Maggie made all of us tough. It's what kept me from going crazy, night after night, doing the same routine, wearing the same disgusting outfits, listening to the same lines from dirty old men and horny little bastards.

I knew she liked me. The other girls knew it too. But it didn't matter. All that mattered was now. Today. The past was the past and it had to stay that way. So, what in the hell was I doing with a box full of the past in the trunk of my car?

At home I had a hundred excuses because I couldn't open the box right away. There were dishes to do, windows to wash, a tiny garden to weed. Homework to do. I even sanded and painted a chair I'd had in my garage for a year. Anything to keep from finding out what my mother thought was so important she needed me to have it after her death.

Errant thoughts occasionally ran through my mind. Letters? Bills? Unsent birthday cards?

It wasn't as if we were close, even before I ran away from home things were never good between us. I tried to talk to her about how my father screamed at her when his dinner was too salty. I struggled to bring up the subject, but she shushed me and told me to pretend it never happened. That's how she always handled stress. She just pretended it never happened. When I ran away, she probably pretended I was still there, right up to the end when she killed my father. Maybe she pretended that never happened, either. Who knows.

Why me?

For two months the box stayed in my living room as I quietly lived my life around it. I went to school. I ate my meals. I did my homework. I left the box alone.

A part of me thought that if I continued to ignore it, that one day maybe the box would just disappear, and I wouldn't have to deal with it. The more realistic part of me said that when I was ready to open it, I'd know.

It was time.

watched a gorgeous sunrise over the ocean then took a long walk along the deserted beach. Sitting on the sand, just out of reach of the lapping waves, I felt a peacefulness surround me. My mind cleared and I knew I was finally ready.

I closed the shutters on my little beach cottage and sat the box on the floor of the living room. Outside, I could hear the waves slapping at the beach. That sound never failed to comfort me. It didn't fail me today, even when I got no comfort from touching the box.

I peeled off the tape imprinted with "Property of State Correctional Facility." It barely kept the flaps together. The box nearly burst with its contents.

I focused on keeping my breathing regular and my shaking hands steady.

Notepads. A box full of notepads. What on earth . . .? I had no idea where to begin. I took them out of the box one by one and started stacking them around me. The piles grew. Piles of plain old legal-size notepads. I couldn't figure out why . . . Why notepads? Then it hit me.

Spiral bound notebooks probably weren't allowed in prison.

My mother's journals.

Her words.

Her life.

I didn't even know my mother liked to write. I knew she read. Magazines mostly. Those True Story magazines about teenage mothers and stuff. She always had a bottle of soda and a bag of potato chips at her elbow when she read those magazines. She'd read them over and over, always wiping her greasy fingers carefully before turning the pages.

I snuck one into the bathroom to read one night, not too long before I ran away. The sad stories intrigued me with their tormented and horrible lives. I didn't think people acted like that in real life and believed the stories were just that - stories.

My mother thought differently. She'd rant and rave about how this person suffered, and that person needed to be punished for hurting so and so. She single-handedly crusaded for the rights of every person in those magazines. I'd hear her talking to herself, mumbling about the strong ones who got away from their attackers. I don't remember much of what she'd say. I tried to ignore her.

I thought hard. There was so much I should remember, and so little that I really did.

Walking home from school; the sun setting behind me. For some reason I can't remember, I got home late. She was mad. She told me to go to the corner store and get a can of tomatoes and a

41

loaf of bread. I hurried as fast as I could, running all the way there and all the way back, but it wasn't fast enough.

She yelled at me for making her late with dinner and mumbled something about getting punished. I thought she meant me. I stayed silent the rest of the night hoping that my father wouldn't ask, and my mother wouldn't tell.

I wasn't punished that night. I never gave it another thought, except that I must have gotten off easy.

Only now, trying hard to remember, I recall the next day my mother had a black eye. She said she fell in the middle of the night tripping over something in the dark. My father called her clumsy all the time. "Accident- prone" were the words he used. Come to think of it, she had a lot of black eyes, and puffy, lips, and . . . my mind shut down. I didn't want to think about this anymore.

A shiver ran through my body.

Maybe that's why it took me so long to finally read my mother's journals. I wish that were true, but deep in my heart I know it wasn't. I was scared to find out what my mother was really thinking.

I made a pot of herbal tea then sat down cross-legged in a small space I managed to create in the midst of the pile of notebooks. With no other sense of direction than just trying to find a logical place to start, I reached out a tentative hand, opened the first journal closest to me, and began to read.

.July 28, 1972 - Too hot to do anything, but did that stop HIM? Of course not. He chooses the hottest day of the summer to decide to work in the yard. It didn't matter that I told him little Charlie would get heatstroke or sunstroke or whatever. He never listens to me. He hasn't listened to me for 17 years, why should he start now? Apparently, my job is to make sure everyone takes breaks, so I fill in for each person taking the break. I tried to explain to him that the only logic in that was that everyone got a break but me, and HIS answer was a quick slap along the right side of my head, of course the kid wasn't around to see it. I should have kept my mouth shut. Now I must work in the heat with a splitting headache. All the while, he walks around like he's king and barks orders at everyone. That poor kid. Even if she happened to do it right the exact way HE wanted, she'd still get yelled at. It's the only kind of communication he knows.

I closed my eyes, trying to remember that hot summer day. I remember lots of summer days working in the yard. My mother beside me, pulling weeds, pushing lawnmowers, raking leaves. I remember complaining about the heat. I remember my father always yelling at us because we just didn't do something to meet his satisfaction. That was the way he was. Afterwards, he usually had something fun planned for us. We'd go to the drive-in and see a movie, or to the lake and go swimming and have a picnic. I guess all kids remember the fun stuff more than the not-so-fun stuff.

I decided to get better organized about reading my mother's journals, so I sorted them by date. I noticed that sometimes it took several notebooks to finish a year, and at other times, one notebook would span a couple of years. I wondered about those times, whether they were lean on words because the times were good, or just the opposite?

By the time I'd finished sorting the journals and gathering pillows and a heavy throw for my "reading nest," the sun was high over the calm, cool ocean. I made a quick lunch of raw vegetables that could easily be munched while I read and snuggled back into my cozy nest.

I struggled through the first few notebooks, deciphering my mother's childish scrawl while trying to imagine this young girl, so happy and in love was the woman who gave birth to me.

I skimmed rather than read too closely my
mother's idealistic ramblings of the sexual prowess
of my father.

I stood up, stretched, and took a quick bathroom
break to distance myself from what I had just read.

Staring at myself in the bathroom mirror, I
silently asked myself if it were possible that
someone else had written these journals.
That maybe, somehow, they were mixed up
with my mother's things while she was in
prison.

The doorbell rang while I contemplated calling the
prison to see if a mix-up were possible.

"Hey, Charlie, ya home?"

That voice could only belong to one person.
Sara. I smiled at her spontaneity. Only Sara
would drive all the way out to Indian Rocks
beach without calling first.

"Hold on, Sara. I'm coming."

I opened the door to behold my friend juggling a
bottle of wine, several Chinese take-out
containers, and a small watermelon.

I rescued the watermelon from splattering on my front walk and led the way into the kitchen.

As we passed my living room, Sara questioned me about the scattered notebooks.

"Working on a new project?"

"No, not really." I took the wine from her and put it in the refrigerator to chill.

"What then? Don't tell me it's homework, cuz I don't remember an assignment, and if I forgot, I'm dead, ok?"

I laughed at the disconcerting look on her face.

"No, it's not homework."

"Girl, you know you can't keep secrets from me, so spill." She opened one of the small white containers and grabbed chopsticks from a drawer. "Shrimp fried rice, yum."

I smiled. Sara was right up to a point.

I took a deep breath and then pursed my lips. I thought about what I should say and then shrugged my shoulders. Someone would find out eventually, I guess it'd be best if I said it first.

I put my arm behind my back and made a mock face of pain. "Oh, ow, okay, I'll tell. Don't twist my arm anymore."

Sara dropped to the floor and sat cross-legged next to one of the piles. Thoughtfully munching her rice, she asked, "Serious stuff, huh?"

I got my own set of chopsticks and opened the other container, beef and broccoli, my favorite, of course. Sara was like that. She took the time to get to know you and then remembered special things, like how much I loved beef and broccoli. And she remembered that when it came to serious stuff, I'd make a joke to get around showing my feelings.

I shoved her over to make room for me and I sat down next to her.

We ate in silence for a few minutes.

"They're my mother's journals."

Sara sat her take out container down and played her chopsticks like a drum. "Ba-da-dum . . . tssh!!" She spoke. "And for my next trick, watch me pull a rabbit out of my hat!"

"I'm serious."

"You said you didn't have a mother. Wait a minute. You told me your mother was dead."

"Well, she is . . . now."

"Wait, are you telling me your mother just died?"

"It's kind of complicated, Sara. You want the short version or the long version?"

Sara smiled and settled back into my comforter. "Oh, definitely the long version, girl." She waved her hand in my general direction. "Speak. I'm listening."

For the rest of the afternoon, I told Sara the story of my life. I didn't leave anything out. When I'd finished, she cried into her paper napkin for a few minutes then composed herself. Sniffling like a child she asked, "Have you read all of these yet?" indicating the piles of notebooks.

"No, I'd just started when you'd arrived."

"Do you mind if I . . . ?" She asked as she tentatively reached a hand toward the closest notebook.

"No, I . . . no, go ahead. I want you to."

48

Sara and I sat and read well into the evening. By the time we'd finished our second pitcher of margaritas, and listened to a rack of jazz CDs twice, we'd finally read the last notebook.

Around sunset, we'd moved out to the back patio to mellow out and give our eyes a rest. Thank goodness I'd had the patio screened last summer, or else we'd been eaten alive by the mosquitoes. The water calmed me while the frogs croaked a soothing reminder that we weren't alone.

I was the first to break the comfortable silence that had settled around us. "I guess I'd turned a blind eye to my parent's relationship."

"How could you have known, Charlie, you were only a kid."

"I must have known something was going on with them back then. I mean, shit, I left home to get away from them, right?"

"Yeah, I know, but according to what your mother wrote, she sheltered you from most of it."

"Not all of it." I mumbled and then quickly changed the subject. "Hey, what about Statistics, huh? You figured out our homework assignment?"

Sara saw right through my diversion. "Fuck Statistics, what did you mean when you said, 'not all of it'?"

This wasn't going to be easy. "I've only told one other person this, Sara. And, well, she promised me that as long as she was alive, he'd never . . . There was this one time, when my father, well . . . he, shit . . . " I flung myself out of my wicker chair and paced nervously. I swung my arms back and forth, trying to wave away bad memories.

"Take your time, girl. Relax. We don't have to do this now, okay?"

I wrapped my arms around my body and squeezed. "I'm ok. I didn't think this would upset me; must be from reading all those notebooks."

I sat back down and turned to Sara. "My father molested me. Once. He came into my room late at night. At first, I thought someone had broken into the house. Then I heard his voice. He said, 'don't ask any questions.' Then he started touching me. I stared into the darkness, I don't even remember if I breathed. When . . . when he was finished all he said was 'don't tell', then he left my room."

Sara gaped at me with her mouth partly open. For once, I'd finally shocked the unshakeable Sara. I went on. "I left home the next day."

Sara and I sat in strained silence, absorbing my words, contemplating our separate lives. A burning sensation began in the pit of my stomach. The fire spread. Heat burned beneath my body's surface. I needed a change.

"Sara."

"mm..hmm?"

"What would you say if I changed my major?"

Sara smirked then said with a tiny bit of

sarcasm, "What major?" Good ol' Sara.

She was back. I could do this.

The End

Black Eyes and Blue Tears

I lay face down on a sun-drenched beach. A deeply tanned stranger with a dark mass of shoulder-length hair strolled toward me. We locked eyes. He knelt next to my towel. A slow smile turned his sharply angled face into a friendly welcome. He offered to rub lotion onto my back. I didn't resist. His strong, capable hands smoothed sunscreen onto my warm, bare skin. I practically purred beneath his touch.

His firm hands gently massaged my tight shoulders. Ah, this was exactly what I needed. I melted under his soothing stroke. I wiggled my backside between his bare legs, begging for more attention.

"Miss Anderson?"

He whispered my name into my ear, his hot breath tickled my hair. I sighed softly. The sharp scent of Hi-Karate burned my nostrils. Absently, I rubbed at my nose.

"Miss Anderson!"

I leaned my head back. Closer to his voice. His breath reminded me of . . . coffee. I wanted to see his dark, smoldering eyes. I opened mine and stared right into – "Professor Stanton!"

The rest of the classroom burst into laughter. A red-hot flush crept up my neck and settled into my cheeks. I didn't need to touch my face to know I looked like I just received an instant sunburn.

"Welcome back, Miss Anderson. Nice trip?"

"Uh . . . I, uh . . . that is, I mean—"

"Yes, well, we know what you mean, Miss Anderson."

"Sir?" Oh, God. Did I say anything embarrassing while I napped?

"You were just going to explain to the rest of the class what the 'law of thumb' meant in the 1700's."

I sunk deep into my chair, wishing I could disappear. Sometimes life just wasn't fair. I prayed for a quick end to my torture. Anything. Flash flood, hurricane, Terrorist attack, I wasn't picky now. A full thirty seconds clicked off the clock before it happened.

"Brrr-rrr-nnnngg"

Saved by the bell! My prayers were answered. End of class. Students sprang from their chairs as if released from tightly wound springs. They bolted for the door. Relief washed over me.

I quickly gathered my books and backpack, then flashed a winning smile at my professor of Sociology. "I'll have to get back to you on that, Professor Stanton."

"You do that, Miss Anderson. I'll look forward to your answer. I'll expect it on my desk tomorrow morning, in no less than five hundred words."

My smile vanished. My shoulders slumped. I cast a furtive glance toward my best friend, Sara. She shrugged her shoulders as if to say, "don't look at me, you were the one caught sleeping."

"Yes, sir."

"Good day, Miss Anderson."

"Yes, sir."

Sara and I filed out of the classroom behind the last of the students and made our way through the crowded hallway into the warm sunshine.

I squinted into the bright sunshine and breathed deep. Classrooms always smelled like dirty feet to me.

"God, I can't believe I fell asleep in class again!"

"What's up with you, girl?" Sara asked as she pulled her backpack off her shoulder and rummaged through it while we walked to the parking lot. Classes over for the day, we planned on spending the rest of the beautiful day on a real beach, not unlike the one I was daydreaming about.

"I dunno." I shrugged as best I could with the weight of my backpack. I guess I deserved that extra assignment Professor Stanton gave me, but he just didn't understand what I was going through lately.

"That's the second time this week, you know. Shit! Where is it." Sara searched frantically through her disorganized bag. "Damn it. Where are they?"

"Sara, why don't we stop for a – Watch out!" I called out to her, but it was too late. She walked right off the edge of the sidewalk and tripped over a small, thin girl sitting on the curb.

"Oh my God, are you ok? Did I hurt you? Bloodied? Bruised?" Sara stood and pulled the girl up with her.

I noticed she wasn't really very young, just small. Fragile popped into my head. I picked up the cause of Sara's distraction and zipped it to prevent Sara's life from scattering.

Sara, oblivious to what she had been searching for, focused her attention on the girl. She smoothed and straightened, brushing bits of grass and gravel from the girl's shirt. "Jeez, I'm sorry, I wasn't watching where I was – my God! Did I do that to you?" Sara held the girl's sleeve and stared at her arm.

"No, please. I'm fine. Leave me alone." She pulled away trying to cover her arms at the same time. Her fingers played at the frayed ends of her shirt, like nervous little butterflies. She ducked her head, refusing to make eye contact

I stared at her arm, too. Both arms. I saw bright blue-black bruises encircling her narrow wrists and arms before they disappeared from my sight, under the worn shirtsleeves. No way Sara had caused that damage. Before I could stop it, a low whistle escaped from my lips.

Ever concerned for wayward puppies and lost souls, Sara, the "touchiest" person I knew, put her hand on the arm of the girl and looked into her eyes. "Oh, girl. You need to get those checked."

"I said I was fine." She pulled her arm away at the same time tossing her long blond hair over her shoulder. She stiffly turned to go. We'd been dismissed.

Sara and I exchanged glances.

"Whatever, okay? I'm sorry about walking into you." Sara took her backpack from me, turned away, and headed for my car. I gave the girl's small, straight back one more look and followed Sara.

Neither of us said anything until we were settled into the front seat of my year-old Mustang convertible enjoying the air-conditioned breeze.

I left the car in park, lowered the thumping tunes coming from the radio, and turned to Sara who had gone back to rummaging in her backpack. "Weird, huh?"

"Yeah. Finally!" She pulled out a pair of sunglasses and held them up in victory. "Yes!"

"Is that what you were looking for?"

"Yep. Gotta look cool in my shades when we're cruising the boulevard in your fine new auto .. mo .. bile." She drew out the last word and tossed me a large, sassy smile as she settled her sunglasses on her tiny, upturned nose and tossed her long curly dark hair. She turned up the radio until I could feel the thumping bass deep down into my very core.

We both laughed at her silly joke. I pressed the button to let the top down. We threw our cares to the wind as we headed for the beach. My best friend was also my weirdest friend, but I wouldn't trade her for anyone else in the world.

The stars in the night sky sparkled like tiny pinpricks of light shining through black construction paper. The moon shined brightly from its high perch above the water.

I curled my legs under me as I sat on a wicker loveseat. I breathed deep of the salty air. It smelled good. A kind of brackish, fishy, sandy smell. Only the Gulf of Mexico had that smell. It smelled like home.

I loved my little beach house. I was far enough from the water to avoid rising water during the occasional storm but close enough to hear the waves lapping at the crushed shells that lined the beach.

I'd finished Professor Stanton's punishing assignment hours ago. I went into lengthy detail about the English common law that decreed a husband had the right to punish his wife with a whip so long as it was no bigger than his thumb, hence the "law of thumb." He should be satisfied that I'd learned my lesson about sleeping in class.

At least, I hope I learned my lesson. God, I had to start getting some sleep. I stretched my legs and leaned back into the cushions. I'd been sitting and listening to the water as I read more of my mother's journals. I couldn't put them down. They were the reason I slept in class.

Night after night I'd reach for them again, re-reading her words, imagining her life. Trying to comprehend the life she lived with my father until she snapped and killed him. What was their existence like? What made her stay? What made him beat her? Why? So many unanswered questions. I probably would never know the real answers. Only hope that I could eventually help others before they ended up like my parents.

I put a lot of my hope into learning as much as I could from my new classes. After I changed my major last month, it was all I could do to keep from plowing ahead of the class material and get to the real situations. So far, all I'd gotten out of the classes were that studying psychology and sociology meant a lot of reading and quoting theories. I wanted real answers. Real answers from real people, not people who'd been dead a hundred years.

###

I pulled into the school parking lot the next morning much earlier than usual.

"Hey!" I shoved my watch into Sara's face. "What's going on? Look at this. We're early!"

Sara pushed my hand out of her face and stuck her tongue out. "Oh, give me a break. I'm not always the one who's late!"

Getting to class early had a great plus I thought as I drove through the parking lot toward the front. I could park a lot closer to the building. Cruising through the first two lanes of cars, I searched for an empty spot. Suddenly, the car in front of me slammed on its brakes. I hit mine too, nearly toppling Sara from her seat.

"Shit!" Sara sputtered. "What's the big idea?"

I threw my hand in front of her to keep her from hitting the dash. "Hang on, this idiot in front of me slammed on the brakes."

"You should have hit him; it'd serve him right."

"Yeah, you say that now, let's see what you say when it's your car. Florida is a 'no-fault' state. I'd have to pay for my own damages."

"Can you get around him?"

"No, he's stopped in the middle of the lane. So much for getting to class early." I tapped my horn hoping to make the person in front of me notice he was blocking the way.

The passenger side door opened, and a cloud of blond hair floated out.
Something familiar about the hair made me take a second look. "Hey, Sara.
Look. It's that girl from yesterday. You know, the one you tripped over."

"Oh yeah, so it is. Huh. Blow your horn again."

"Wait, look." I motioned for Sara to watch. The girl leaned into the car, as if to get a kiss goodbye. Instead, she was hit full, across the face by the man behind the wheel.
Sara and I both gasped at the same time. We turned to each other, amazed at what we just saw. "Did you –"

"Did he just –"

We both started talking then stopped at the same time. "Incredible." I spoke.

"I can't believe that just happened." Sara held a hand to her lips as if feeling for the sting of the slap the other girl received.

I slammed my hand down on my horn and let it wail. The blonde turned quickly and then said something to the man in the car. He flung his hand out his side window and sent a single finger gesture in our direction.

Sara opened her window and yelled, "Oh, big man. Beat up little girls. Move your fuckin' car!"

Between my horn blowing and Sara's mouth, we'd drawn a little crowd. I could see the blond gesturing to the man in the car. It looked like she was trying to get him to stay in the car and leave.

Adrenalin pounded through my veins. I almost wanted him to get out of his car and threaten us. I blew the horn again, just for good measure. The blonde turned and looked at me. Her eyes wide with fear. I let go of the horn. Something inside of me twisted.

"Sara," I said without losing eye contact.

"Huh?"

"Get out and go make sure she's all right. Get her away from the car. And Sara, don't you go near that car." I added. I knew Sara would intervene if it got ugly. I wanted to find a parking spot quickly.

"You got it. That son-of-a-bitch isn't going to hit her again."

"Sara."

She stopped to turn as she shut the door. "Charlie don't worry. I'm not going to do anything stupid. Neither is he. Not with all these witnesses."

"Be careful."

"I will. Go park the car. We'll be waiting for you by the fountain."

###

I could see Sara sitting next to the girl with the blonde hair and a small crowd around them. Sara still looked furious. I hurried over.

"Hey," I motioned to Sara. "I waited and parked my car after I watched that guy leave campus. She all right?" I tilted my head in the direction of the girl staring at the ground. She didn't even lift her head to acknowledge that we were talking about her.

"Yeah. I think so. Sherilynn, meet Charlie."

"Hi, Sherrilyn." I put out my hand to shake hers. No response. Maybe it was the crowd. I turned around and addressed the curious group that had gathered. "Hey, why don't ya'll just go on and leave us alone. There's nothing to see."

As soon as the last of the lingering crowd wandered away, I heard a small voice. "Thank you."

"You're welcome. Do you need to go to a hospital or something?"

"No, I'll be all right." Sherrilyn gently touched her face. She winced as her fingers met the swollen flesh. I watched a vacant look pass over her crystal- blue eyes. Something inside of me told me that this wasn't the first time she'd been hit.

Sara was more direct and to the point. "Who was that son-of-a-bitch? Your husband? Has he hit you before? Should we call the police?"

Sherilynn shrank from Sara's demanding barrage of questions. She shook like a scared rabbit caught in a snare.

"Sara." I placed a calming hand on her shoulder. She got the message. "Why don't you head into class, and I'll stay with Sherrilyn for a few minutes, okay?"

Sara exchanged a long look with me before she grabbed her backpack and headed toward the double doors. This wasn't over. I knew Sara.

"There, now we got rid of the crowd. We'll just sit here for a few minutes until you calm down." I wanted to put her at ease as quickly as possible. Desperately, I searched my mind for past lessons about dealing with abuse victims. I could help her if I could just remember what to do.

We sat in silence. Students wandered past us without a glance. We were just two more students lingering outside the building before classes started. The splash of the fountain was mesmerizing, and I stared at it lost in the rhythmic spray waiting for the girl beside me to stop shaking.

"Sherilynn, has this happened before?" I kept my voice intentionally soft and low. It made her pay attention.

She lifted her head. Tears trailed down her cheeks. Her blue eyes still vacant. Tears shimmered like clear blue drops. What was she thinking?

"My husband Ray . . . he loves me, ya know." She spoke with a thick southern accent. She must be a native Floridian – a rare breed. She clasped her hands tightly in her lap.

"Does he show you he loves you like this a lot?"

"He's letting me take these classes here so I can get me a better job."

"Sherrilyn, look at me, honey." I took her cold hands in mine. "Has your husband hit you before?" A tiny spark of recognition flickered in her eyes. The dark shadows already appearing. She was going to have one heck of a black eye.

"He hits me all the time." She whispered with quivering lips.
"Do you want him to stop?"

"I want him to -- " She stopped talking and stared over my shoulder.

"Sherilynn! Git your ass in this car, right now."

"Ray wants me. I gotta go." She patted the concrete bench checking for anything she may have left behind.

"Sherrilyn, wait, I can help you." I wanted her to stay away from this man. He meant nothing but trouble for her; I knew it. I wanted to get her help.

"Sherilynn, don't make me come and git you." His voice growled as he made his threat.

Sherrilyn hurried to her feet and looked over her shoulder at me as she started to walk away. "You can't help me. No one can." Then, with contrite in her voice, she called to her husband, "I'm coming, Ray."

I watched in horror as he grabbed her by the upper arm and threw her up against the car door as if he wanted to throw her through it. He was at least a foot taller than Sherilynn and a good hundred pounds heavier.

I stood quickly and half-stepped toward them. Sherrilyn must have seen me or sensed that I would follow. She called out to me. "Charlie, don't. I'm okay. I just fell, that's all."

"That's right, leave us alone. My wife is one clumsy klutz. She's falling, all the time."

He yanked open the car door and tossed the girl into the front seat as if she were a package. He could have cared less if the package had 'fragile' written all over it. I had a decision to make.

I kept my eye on the light blue car while I ran to mine. I would follow them for a short distance; just to make sure Sherilynn was all right. If I saw anymore abuse, I'd phone the police from my cellphone.

I followed the car out of the parking lot and into traffic. I doubt if they even noticed I was behind them, so intent they were in their argument. However, it looked like he was doing most of the yelling and gesturing while she merely sat, taking it all. Each time he gestured vigorously, the car weaved in its lane.

I thought about the other cars on the road, drivers oblivious to the drama going on in the light blue sedan ahead of me. He'd better start paying attention to his driving or else he'd cause an accident.

I felt so sorry for her. Was this what my mother went through? Was Ray a younger image of my father?

A fire ignited inside of me. I had to help this girl. I couldn't let her become another statistic.

I

Hope flared when I saw the car pull into a convenience store. Ray went inside while Sherrilyn sat in the car. I parked my car then knocked on her window. She jumped in fright, saw it was me, and rolled down her window.

"What are you doing here?" She kept watching the front door of the store. I knew she was watching for her husband.

"Sherilynn, I couldn't live with myself if something happened to you. Would you let me help you?

"Charlie, you don't understand. Ray's not like this all the time. Really. He just, oh . . . God, here he comes. Go on now, leave before he gets here."

"Sherrilyn, you can come with me. I'll take you to the police, or to a shelter. Whatever you want." I couldn't let her go. A voice inside of me pushed harder. "I don't want anything to happen to you." My voice rose as I felt the anxiety crawl inside of me.

"Hey, git away from my car!" Ray's voice boomed loudly in my ear. He stood close to me, trying to intimidate me with his size. My heart pounded in my chest, but my blood boiled. He wouldn't dare hit me.

I kept one hand on the car door and looked him straight in the eye. "Your wife is my friend. I'm trying to help her. You don't have any right to hit her." I deliberately kept my voice even, speaking each sentence clearly. I had to show him he couldn't control me.

"Look, I don't know who you are, but this is between me and my wife." He spat the last word out as if it left a bad taste in his mouth. As an afterthought, he tossed Sherilynn a small packet of frozen peas. "Put that on your face."

"Charlie, don't get involved." Sherrilyn whispered from her seat in the car. She touched my hand once with her icy fingers. The other hand gently pressing the cold bag to her swollen, black eye. "I'll be all right. Honest." She attempted a smile. "Ray, here is all calmed down. We worked things out. Right, honey?" She reached out to tentatively put her hand on his arm. I watched, thinking it was as if she were reaching her hand toward a rabid animal, scared it might bite her.

"That's right, babe." He patted her hand in what he must have thought was a loving gesture.

I tore a scrap of paper from a notebook and quickly jotted down my telephone number. I pressed the scrap into Sherrilyn's hand. "Call me if you need to talk."

I

I gave her husband a hard, intense look and said, "I'll see you on campus tomorrow, Sherilynn."

"Sure thing, Charlie. I'll be there." Her voice too high, too forced. I stared at the spot their car was in, long after it left the convenience store. I feared that I had just seen the last of Sherrilyn.

###

Coffee cup in hand, I stepped out into the early morning mist for the newspaper. I breathed deeply of the wet, salty air. The gulf fog hung low over the trees. Mornings like this made me feel so isolated, so alone.

I tossed the newspaper onto the table and settled into a chair. My cup stalled half-way to my lips as I read the front headlines: "Murder-Suicide ends in fiery, fatal crash."

My insides went cold. My hand shook as I placed the coffee cup back on the table, sloshing coffee onto the paper.

I read the entire article twice before calling Sara. She picked up on the first ring as if she were expecting my call.

"Sara," my voice trembled. "Did you read the paper yet?

Yeah, I did. It was her, wasn't it?"

"Yes.

"He killed her didn't he?"

"That's what the paper said. Oh God, Sara. I tried to get her to come with me. I should have tried harder!" I slammed my hand down on the paper, covering the picture of the smashed blue car, half burned wrapped around a pole.

"Charlie, you can't blame yourself."

I sobbed into the phone. "I could have helped her. I should have insisted she get in my car."

"Then he would have killed both of you."

"So, are you saying my life was worth more than hers?"

"No, not at all. Charlie, I understand you're upset. But listen. You couldn't force her any more than he had a right to hit her."

"But it's not the same."

73

I

"Yes, it is. You can't help her if she doesn't want help. Besides, you had no idea that it was going to get that violent."

"Sara?"

"Yeah, hon?"

"I'm not going to let the next one go so easily."

"That's my girl."

The End

Please Don't Go

"Mommy, where is daddy going?"

"Away." My mother didn't turn away from the sink as she washed dishes. The sun streamed in through the kitchen window making her hair shine is if made from gold.

I ran to the door. "Daddy!"

Daddy stopped, put down his suitcase, turned to me. "Come here." He knelt on one knee, opening his arms.

I rushed to him and threw my chubby little arms around his neck. Patting the blonde curls atop my head, he kissed my face and told me to be a good girl. I kissed him back and begged him not to go. I held his hand tight between my two small ones as he walked to the door.

"Good-bye, baby." Daddy didn't look at me.

"Bye, daddy." I followed him out the door and watched from my seat on the stoop as he put his suitcase in the trunk of the car then climbed behind the wheel.

The car engine roared with anger. I winced at how loud it sounded.

I

I waved.

Daddy waved back. Then he was gone.

"Please don't go daddy," I whispered.

###

A dark evening, twenty-eight years later, my small son said, "Mommy, where is daddy going?"
    heard the question but didn't know how to
            answer. I cuddled my little boy
close. I breathed deep of his special baby smell trying to commit it to memory. I wanted to block out the rest of the day and only remember this one single moment holding my son close to my heart.

"I'm packed."

I looked up to see my husband with a suitcase in his hand a garment bag over his shoulder.

I nodded, afraid to use my voice.

"Daddy, please don't go."

My husband knelt to absently brush away a wisp of golden hair from my son's forehead. "I have to, son." He patted his arm. "You be a big boy and take care of mommy."

Such a large load of responsibility for a tiny boy. I pulled him back into the safety of my arms. I whispered into his ear, "Well take care of each other." He snuggled closer, "you promise you won't leave?" He asked with his child-like innocence.

"Never. Ever." I crossed my heart. "We'll be together forever."

He turned in my arms and buried his face in my bosom. I held him tight as his father walked out the door. In the tiniest whisper, I heard him say, "Daddy, please don't go."

###

One day, thirty years later, I couldn't stop myself from crying out, "Oh mama, please don't go!" I held her fragile hand tightly in mine. The sun shone through the bedroom window and created a soft halo of light around her head. Her pale, white hair luminescent against the pillow.

"Hush darling, It's my time." My mama whispered the words as I leaned closer to hear her.

"I'm going to miss you so much. Don't leave me."
"I'll never leave you." She ran her fingers through my hair like she did when I was a child. I'll always

be with you." Her bony fingers shook as she touched my chest above my left breast. "Right here." Mama drew a shallow breath and sighed, "always."

Tears swam in my eyes, as I watched my mother take her last breath.

"Oh mama, please don't go," I whispered.

###

For as long as I could, I breathed in and out hoping to never hear my son cry out those lonely words. I lost the battle seventeen years later.

"Mama, please don't go!"

My son had grown into a tall, handsome man. I loved hm so much. My heart, heavy in my chest, ached for him. "Don't cry, baby."

"Mama, you can't leave. You promised to be with me forever." His face, although lined with age, still held a boyish glow in the afternoon sun that streamed in from the window across from my bed.

"Darling, how could I ever leave my baby boy?" I touched his beautiful face. I held tight to my delicate grasp on life. I pulled him close to my chest and lay his head on a bosom long dried and useless. I gently brushed at the lock of sandy hair that continued to fall over his brow. His tears pierced through my thin cotton gown, straight into my heart.

"I love you, mama." My son sobbed as he held me tighter than I could ever hold him again.

"I'm sorry, son."

"For what, mama?" He hiccupped then took a deep breath.

As I closed my eyes, I gently touched his strong hand with my dried wrinkled one. "For breaking my promise."

The End

Silver Screen Escape

The front porch of my childhood home wasn't a porch at all. It was more like a stoop, or just a step. Made of concrete and about eight inches high, it separated the front yard from the front door. To everyone else it was just the front step, but to me it was much more; it was where I perched my bottom on the cold concrete and waited. At first, I didn't know what I was waiting for, only that I didn't have it.

I sat on the front stoop and watched cars drive by, restricted from going any further away from the familiar confines of my home. As I grew older, I sat and waited for friends to come over to play, or for parents to visit on "their day."
Hundreds and hundreds of days came and went with visits, and later with disappointments when the clock ticked away until I could no longer deny that no car would pull into the driveway with a parent to swoop in and take me away. On that stoop I dreamed, and I waited for my chance to escape.

With an overwhelming sense of understanding beyond my young years, I knew I didn't belong. I didn't fit into the life I'd been born. I only existed, floating between the other lives that continued around me. Born to a mother who couldn't love my father, she married another who gave me his name. Parents and stepparents drifted in and out of my life, so much so that I lost track of their names and faces. Nothing was real except the unknown desire to escape growing inside of me.

My pursuit for escape took a dramatic turn in the early 1970s. Escape encompassed my desire to disappear--disappear from my family, my school, but most of all from my life. Unsure of how to fulfill my desire, I searched for a solution to what I envisioned as my problem.

It didn't take too long to discover the key. It appeared almost as if by magic. Eager, excited, and full of anticipation, I watched it take shape. For many months from the window of my school bus, I kept an eye on the builders as they moved concrete blocks around and poured cement. First the foundation, then the walls, and finally a roof appeared as if right before my eyes. Large glass doors and plate glass windows gave the building a wide, gaping, friendly look that seemed to say, "Come in. I'm here for you." The two small windows where tickets were sold balanced out the smiling face. Unblinking, they beckoned to me, "Come in. I'm here for you." I knew it was meant for me.

Opening day arrived. I paced, checking the time every few minutes until I could find an excuse plausible enough to satisfy the adults. Rushing to the door, I reigned in my excitement, certain that if my joy were detected, it would be taken away. As casually as I could, I opened the front door, stepped onto the front stoop, and closed the door behind me. My spine stretched tight as I waited for any noise from inside to call me back. I took the first tentative step off the stoop. Slowly at first, then gaining in speed, I covered more ground across the lawn. Out of the driveway and finally on the road, I could start to relax. I was on my way.

I walked the two miles to the first walk-in movie theater in our town. The two miles seemed insurmountable, although with each step I knew it brought me closer to my destination. I kicked at gravel along the side of the road and swiped at waist-high weeds along the ditch. With each kick I wished I were already standing in line for my ticket. With each swipe I willed myself to already be sitting in my seat.

I spent most of my summers as a teen huddled in a soft seat in the darkened theater staring up at the wide screen. Nearly every weekend you could find me in the cool dark shadows, far away from the realities of divorce, stepparents, and becoming a teenager. In the theater I didn't have to think, only see.

I absorbed every horror film shown, devouring them repeatedly. I couldn't get enough of the creepy, campy horror films of the early 1970s. No matter that I had nightmares every night, I was addicted. They were my antithesis. I endured life knowing the dark theater with its visual trips to faraway places would comfort me in times of need.

The characters in the movies became an extension of my identity. In observing their evil deeds, I could manifest my desires through them. I watched a young boy train rats to attack people in *Willard*, and then watched *Ben* do the same. Not truly understanding the significance, I pretended that those in my life who hurt me would end up in the same predicament. They would pay for their misdeeds.

Trainable animals gave way to intelligent vehicles. My appetite for horror was voracious. Just like the gasoline truck in *Duel* plowed through people, I plowed my way through more and more films. It was when I first saw *Carrie* that I understood my reasons for watching these shocking shows. Here was someone that dispensed justice to those who harmed her. I silently rooted for Carrie, while those in the theater around me were frightened.

My life took on a new twist when I graduated high school. I found a new escape from that small house with the small stoop—living. Graduation from high school was more than just a transition between childhood and adulthood. It was a release, an opportunity for me to oversee my own life and destiny.

I had survived my childhood. The adult role models I had weren't the greatest, but are any role models ever perfect? Sure, they let me down, but they didn't bring me down. Through life's lessons I learned positive coping mechanisms that will carry me through the rest of my days. Did I make mistakes? You bet I did. And with each mistake I learned and grew, making the most of my opportunities rather than hiding away, stunted like a plant kept in the dark. It was hard, but I never gave up.

The theater is still there, although it no longer shows first-run films. Age has caught up with my once favorite refuge, just as it has caught up with me. Wrinkles on my face and the gray in my hair mirror the cracks in the building's concrete surface as it shines dully in the sun showing pits and broken cinder blocks.

It's been a very long time since I sought to escape and find refuge using horror films or theaters. Today I write my dreams in journals. I no longer ache to escape a dreary life, but to embrace its beauty. I've bloomed from that once diminutive plant I was to a strong, sturdy flowering bush reaching higher. Every morning, I thank God for having one more day to live, and every evening I thank God for giving me that day. I am grateful to

a small hometown theater for rescuing me before I
ever got the opportunity to understand that life
truly is precious.

The End

Boot Camp Serious

We stood at attention for so long I thought I'd break down from heat stroke. Finally, our sergeant gave us the parade rest command.

Heaven.

A light breeze picked up. I stretched my short body as high as I could to catch the intermittent wind as it passed by. We were packed in like sardines. All of us sweating, dripping on each other.

Those at the head of the squad received the command to pick of the backpacks on the ground and help put them on the recruits in front of them. Then signal to the recruit behind that they were ready for their backpack. At once, forty pounds heavier, the world took on a new meaning.

A silence fell over the squad. Then the next squad. Then the next. No more jocularity. We didn't even complain about the weather.

Life just became serious.

The End

Red, White & Blue Peace

The trade embargo and travel restrictions lifted, peace seemed eminent for the two countries: the United States and Cuba. So different; yet so close One tiny country; a mere 90 miles from the much larger one. Both had seen the industrial revolution change their futures; both had seen too much death occur for the sake of their peoples' rights.

The President of the United States stood with his First Lady, smiles on their faces; relaxed and jubilant. Their dream now a reality. They talked of heroes and moments in history. His would be the name in the books next to the title, "United States at Peace with Cuba."

The President of Cuba, regal in his full military dress stood to one side: his aides attending to him. Arrogance surrounded this man still even though he had been the one to sacrifice the most for peace. He stood stiff as a board. Proud. He too, thought of history. A history of power. A history of people. His power gone. His people no longer cheered for him. A figurehead, the United States press called him. Akin to England's Queen. He impatiently waved his attendants away. He stood alone, stiff and proud; yet he felt shamed in front of his own people.

Secret Service agents drifted about the room; busy and efficient. Earpieces abuzz, filled with last minute instructions.

It would only be a few minutes more before the presidents made their first joint appearance to the world. A large crowd had gathered for this momentous occasion. Protection for both presidents was uppermost in the minds of each guard stationed at strategic points.

Music from a band of Cuban musicians filtered through the open window.
The President of Cuba himself had chosen them to play for this event.
Hearing the happy tune, he relaxed his stance a bit, a toe tapping lightly.

The Secret Service Agent in Charge raised his hand. The signal given, he gathered the two Presidents, and the First Lady like a mother hen hovering over a brood.

"This is it, Mr. President."
"That's great, Baker. Good job."

"Thank you, Mr. President" He held his finger to his earpiece, receiving last minute reports. "Okay, the area is secure. We can go."

The President of the United States, his wife on one side, and the President of Cuba on the other, stepped out into the sunshine. The crowd, waving and cheering, swelled behind the containment ropes.

Pop! Pop!

Screams from the crowd.

Pop! Pop! Pop!

The musicians, unaware of shots fired, played on. The piano player lifted a hand to wipe away a stream of sweat, his hand covered in blood. Only then did he discover a bullet had grazed his head. He stood, stumbled a step, then two, and fell.

The First Lady struggled to free herself from her assigned Secret Service agents. Her tailored blue suit with the white ruffled collar, covered in thick red blood. She didn't want to follow protocol. She wanted to get to her husband. "Let me go. Let me see him!"

Instead of abiding her commands, the agents surrounded her and pulled her back into the safety of the room they had just exited.

"My husband! You must let me see my husband." The First Lady pleaded, while she

tore at the Secret Service agent's arm as he
held her, pulling her away from the door.

"Ma'am," the agent held her in place. "The other
agents will get him. Stay here!"

Screams echoed through the room from the crowd
outside.

Sirens shrieked.

Bullhorns blared instructions to the hysterical
crowd.
Running footsteps outside the room mixed with the
shouts, orders and responses.

The First Lady stood alone, waiting in her blue
suit, covered in red blood, fear clutching her
heart as her white gloved hands grasped
together in silent prayer

Whose blood? Her husband's or the Cuban
President's?

Both?

Alone, she waited.

The End

Indian Giver

No one knows how or why she started her skid. It could have been the whiskey or the pills. Maybe both. It could have been all those kids. People say she gave up. Went bad. Lost her mind.

She was trying to kill the dreams. That's what I think. Everyone dreams. Has dreams. Hopes. Desires. You wouldn't be human if you didn't have dreams. But her dreams were different. Why? Because they didn't come true. Not one of them.

So, not everyone's dreams come true. What was her problem? She wasn't all that special, right? But she was.

She is.

Because she is me.

And I lost a piece of myself each time one of my dreams didn't come true.
Every time. I came apart little by little. It wasn't even enough to notice at first. If I had noticed, maybe I would have done things different. You know, made other choices.

But I didn't. So, I didn't.

But, come apart I did. In a big way.

What were my dreams, you ask? Nothing spectacular. Not to me. Maybe not to anyone. I wanted to make a difference in the world. That's what I dreamed. To be someone important. Someone other people looked up to. I dreamed of holding life in the palm of my hand and nurturing it, then giving it to a grateful world.

But some would say I already did that. Already gave life. Gifted the world. I had a baby. Babies. Four of them before my body got so stretched and worn out that he threw me away. Discarded, like old garbage. Tossed out on the curb. Forgotten.

Were those babies my gift to the world? God, I hope not. Not those kids. Liars, cheaters, thieves, and murderers. All of them. Not a good one in the bunch.

My fault.

What could I have done differently? What should I have done? Does it even matter now? With each kid I dreamed that this one would be different. This one would be the one to make a change for the better.

Yeah, like my dreams were going to come true.

Each kid started out good. At least that's what I tell myself in the cold dark nights when I can't close my eyes and can't find relief from the voices. Was it enough that I tried? Or didn't I try enough?

Are children a product of their family or their environment? Maybe it's both. I thought I raised them right. At least I did the best I could considering the circumstances. That's what I thought. Maybe I didn't. Circumstances can change. Would it have mattered?

Their father wasn't there for them. And when he was, it was more for the beatings he inflicted on us on a regular basis than for the advice he hammered into our heads about "never amounting to nothing." He was good at that. Giving advice. Almost as good as the punches and the kicks he doled out to whomever ended up closest to him during one of his outbursts.

It was usually me. I guess I just didn't know any better. Was I trying to protect my kids? I can't remember.

The schools didn't take any notice. But then, I guess I shouldn't have expected them to.

It takes a village.

Right.

The gangs got them first. Then jail. They always learned something new in jail. Maybe their father was right

Look at me now.

Take a good look.

Here I am, laying in my own puke, strapped to a hard bed, in a windowless room, waiting for anyone to wander by. Maybe actually come by my room and see me.

Somebody.

Anybody.

How did I get here, you ask? It all started when I went looking for a way to stop the voices. You know. The doctors explained to me that those voices in your head are supposed to tell you how good you are. What a great person you are and what you're doing is right and warn you when you're going to do something wrong.

Well, mine aren't that nice.

Mine ridicule me. Make fun of me. Torture me with their rants and screaming accusations. It's dark and twisted inside of my head. Evil voices. Wicked thoughts. I know that.

Now.

The drinking started first. Just a glass in the evenings that later slipped into two or three. Before I knew it, I substituted my morning coffee for a warm amber glass of whiskey. A better pick up than caffeine and I liked the buzz I got from drinking on an empty stomach. Whole days ceased to exist. I remember waking up, but it got foggy by the afternoon. The empty bottles of whiskey accumulated in the garbage but there always seemed to be a full bottle on the counter.

Like magic.

My own little booze fairy.

The refrigerator stayed empty, but the booze bottles never slowed.

Who was I to question?

For a while it worked. You know. The voices. They weren't so loud. Sometimes for a little while they weren't so naughty. Quiet. But they always came back.

Always.

Eventually the booze wasn't enough. Of course, the voices knew before I knew. They always did. And they told me where to find the pills.

It was easy.

I guess kids are good for something after all.

Those mind-numbing little red pills, and the white ones too. They both worked. Even better when I used them together. They slid right down with a good swallow of whiskey.

Why take them?

Why not?

Am I looking for sympathy? Not hardly. I don't deserve your sympathy. Not anymore. Probably not ever. Not after what I did. No one feels sorry for me anyway

What did I do, you ask? If I tell you, you'll hate me too. They all hate me.

I didn't plan it, you know. My lawyer says that's a plus for my side. What does he know? He doesn't feel sorry for me either. Although, I didn't really expect him to. He's only here because the state requires it. He told me so.

I guess what I did was expected, considering I'd been hearing those voices for so long. I'm not surprised, really. Not now, anyway. Nothing surprises me now. I guess not after what I did.

You really want to know, don't you?

You know how when you're a kid you give something away, like one of your toys and then you want it back? They call you an Indian Giver. I never gave anybody anything I wanted back.

Until then.

So, I took it back. All four of them. My accidental gifts to the world. It was easy. Guns had a way of appearing in our house. Here and there. No one noticed when I took one. They rarely paid attention to me anyway. I showed them. I just didn't expect so much blood.

Some people call me a monster. Maybe I am. Maybe that's how those rotten kids got that way in the beginning. Conceived by a monster. I don't think they were supposed to be here in the first place. They weren't meant to be born.

Not from me. Not with him.

But who knows.

It doesn't really matter now, does it?

The End

The Sea Haiku

Undersea is life
Mystery to those above
Separate yet same

Drifting on current
Fins flutter, here and then gone
Fish swim in the sea

Slow pulsing coral
Gently waving in rhythm
Feeding with filters

Scuttle and scatter
Little crabs travel about
Sandy bottom; hide

Yellow, blue, purple
Colors brilliant below
Beautiful undersea

Why can't I hide here?
Far below the surface glare
Ocean beautiful

But sea not for me
Wonders lost; me too
I walk by the sea

The End

Who is Making that Awful Racket?

Carrie hummed to the contemporary music coming from her stereo while she dusted the various articles in her tiny living room. She hummed to Adele while she dusted the curio cabinet. She did a a bit of a dance step when she moved on to the large wooden coffee table. Her duster swiftly collected the tiny dust particles while her collection of seaside sculpture gleamed.

She stumbled when over the soft crooning of Maroon 5, and Adam Levine's silky voice, blared an obnoxious noise that could only be described as the last painful wails of a dying animal.

Moose? Not in this part of the city. Carrie dismissed the thought.

A dying cat? Possibly. She opened her apartment door to investigate, praying she didn't find any animal in the last throes of death on the welcome mat outside her door.

The racket continued in the hall. She followed it as it grew louder outside an apartment that was empty only a day or so ago. With a breath of self-confidence, she didn't feel completely to her feet, she doubled her fist and knocked firmly on the door awaiting an encounter with her neighbor, the alleged torturer or killer of small animals.

She didn't have a chance to second guess herself. The door opened quicker than she expected. Face to face with her new neighbor, her jaw dropped. The man in front of her stood at least seven feet tall with a stomach that fell over the top of his pants and matched his barrel chest that must have been as big as a large beer keg.

She rubbed her ears; at least the painful racket had stopped. What are you doing in there? Carrie couldn't believe her audacity. She gestured to the room behind the mountain of a man standing in her way.

"You don't appreciate the works of the great Richard Wagner?

Carried stared back with a blank look.

The greatest opera composer of the nineteenth century?" The man harrumphed with his brash foghorn voice.

"I don't' appreciate offensive noise or you making a racket so I can't even enjoy my day off, no, I don't." Carried stood on her tip toes to give her more leverage that her original five feet of height. It didn't work. Knees shaking, she backed away slowly. "Can you just keep it down?" With a squeak, not of her own volition, she added, "please?"

"You will come to love the opera, my dear girl, you will," the big man bellowed after her retreating figure.

She made her way back to her apartment, shut the door and slumped against it. *Not in this lifetime*. The retort came late, but it didn't matter. She was home.

Peace and quiet.

As abrupt as it had ended, the caterwauling started again, louder than before.

Opera, indeed. Carrie snorted. She may not ever see an opera in her lifetime; however, she did know good music.

That noise was not it.

Carrie slid to the floor, back against her door. In her mind, she attempted to calculate the number of hours she would need to work to soundproof her apartment. An extra 50 or 100 hours, on her salary? Until then, she would do what any good city apartment dweller would do in a situation like this.

She bounced to her feet, reached her entertainment center and turned up her stereo.

No more cat killing screeching and wailing for her.

The End.

Six Word Memoirs

Living humbly; life good for you.

The credits have rolled. The End.

You: Tour Guide for your Life.

Do you love the you today?

Fast and furious: Life changes quickly.

Do you trust your own fear?

Hearts flutter from heaven sent angels.

Flag folded. Tears fall. Rifle fires.

The End

One Word Sentence

Bang.

Speculation:

Was it the beginning? The starter's pistol? Was it the end? A suicide? A sniper's rifle. Was it a firework celebration? You decide. I already know the answer.

The End

Lightning Response

Henry and Selma Higgins retired to a small, assisted living community on the shores of the Gulf of Mexico, not far from Tampa. Henry, being the more mobile of the two, spent much of his day wandering the neighborhood, picking up gossip, and managing to stay out of trouble - only just.

Selma looked forward to Henry's walks because it got him out of her way. She loved the man dearly but wished at times he would cease his endless prattling. Take this morning, for instance. Selma busied herself by cleaning up after breakfast while Henry followed her like a puppy begging for attention.

"Selma, did I tell you what old man Patterson said yesterday?"

"Yes, dear."

"Did I tell you that he's been keeping company with that widow down the way?"

"Yes, dear." Selma said.

"Did I tell you—"

"Henry Wallace Higgins! For crying out loud, will you find something to do? God should strike you down for wagging that gossipy old tongue!"

Henry mumbled about only wanting to pass on some news as he kept a fair distance from Selma's sharp tongue.

"Henry, don't you pay no never mind to what that old rogue Patterson does. I don't know what's worse, the two of you old men together out causing trouble or you both on your own, getting into twice as much!"

Selma turned at a quick knock on the door. "Speak of the devil."

"Hey, Higgins, come on out. Gotta show you sumpin' out here!"

Henry looked to Selma.

"Oh, go on with you. It'll get you out from under my feet. Just don't get into any more trouble!"

With an excited yelp, Henry grabbed his hat, pecked Selma on the cheek and headed for the door before she changed her mind.

Wiping off the counter, Selma dropped the rag and held a hand to her mouth to suppress a giggle. "That old man will never grow up."

She settled into her easy chair with a glass of sweet tea and her favorite magazine. Halfway through an interesting story, she jumped nearly six feet while dropping her magazine when Henry bounded through the door wheezing and out of breath.

Holding a hand over her heart she gasped, "Good Lord, you gave me such a fright!"

Henry collapsed on the small couch; mimicking Selma's hand clutched to her chest. "You should have seen us, Sel. "

Wheeze.

"We found this snake in

the laundry room."

Cough.

"And set it loose in the rec room."

Gasp. This was from Selma.

Henry's eyes watered as he laughed like a little boy.

"Henry Wallace Higgins, God should strike you down for all those practical jokes you play!"

The next morning, Selma and Henry sat quietly as they listened to the pastor's sermon about the power of the Almighty God. Afterwards, they filed out of the church with the rest of the congregation. The parking lot emptied fast. By the time Henry and Selma paid their respects to the pastor, only a few cars were left.

Henry held Selma's arm as he walked at her side, slowing his eager steps to her more hesitant ones.

"Selma," Henry kept his voice low. "Old man Patterson and I want to___"

###

Selma blinked and shielded her eyes. She struggled to sit up only to find herself being held down by a man in a fireman's uniform. "What happened?" she asked, confused as to why her voice sounded so far away.

"Near as we can figure, ma'am, a lightning strike."

"Henry?"

"He's fine too, ma'am. We're going to take you both to the hospital and get you checked out."

Familiar laughter drifted across to Selma's ringing ears. *How could that old fool be laughing at a time like this?*

The old man's body shook as he laughed. Those in the crowd murmured that the shock had caused him to lose his mind. For whom in their right mind would laugh after being struck by lightning?

The first set of paramedics helped him to a stretcher while the others helped poor Selma. As they lay side by side in their separate stretchers, Selma held out her small, bony hand toward Henry. She shook a finger at him, "See, I told you that God would strike you down!"

Henry continued to laugh.

"What are you laughing at, old man?" Selma demanded. Her voice hoarse and scratchy.

"You, old woman!"

Selma stared back in disbelief. "What?"
"God didn't strike me down; he was aiming at you!"

"Why you old . . . "Selma had no words to describe her outrage.

"See what you get for telling Him what to do all the time!" With a final burst of laughter, the old man lay back on his stretcher and motioned with his hand for the paramedics to put him into the ambulance.

The End

Just The Way You Like It

"What the hell is the bucket and mop doing in front of the door?"

Sue cringed. "Hank? Is that you?"

"Who were you expecting, the Pope?" Hank stomped through the small laundry room that separated the garage from the kitchen. White dusty flecks of drywall compound scattered over the spotless linoleum.

Sue pressed her lips tight. In silence she followed behind her husband with the dust mop making his tracks disappear. "How was your day?"

Hank sank into his recliner and punched the remote control. Loud laughter from the audience of a talk show filled the room. "Damn, woman. You been messing with my clicker again?"

Sue said nothing but hurried to change the TV to Hank's favorite fishing program.

Leaning back, he kicked off one boot and then other in the general direction of the coffee table. Thick, sticky globs of still soft drywall compound ground into the carpet beneath his heavy boots. "When's dinner?"

Scrubbing the carpet with a wet rag, Sue looked up. "In about an hour, Hank." In a lower tone she added, "just like it always is."

Shoving a sweat-soaked foot in Sue's face, Hank ordered her to take off his socks while she was down there.

Sue peeled the thick material from Hank's feet. Cold white, wrinkled flesh dotted with bright red angry sores appeared. Sue swallowed hard to keep herself from gagging. From years of working heavy construction, Hank's feet had paid the price.

Without waiting to be told, Sue squeezed a quarter-sized dollop of gray paste from the half-used tube of generic zinc oxide. Closing her eyes to the sight, she smoothed the thick substance over each foot, covering the rashes.

"Get me a beer, will ya?" Hank leaned back in his chair and propped his greasy feet on the ottoman.

Before getting up, Sue lifted Hank's feet and put a newspaper underneath to keep the zinc oxide from getting on the heavy material.

Irate, Hank kicked the paper onto the floor. "Whatcha doing? That white crap gets all over the paper and leaves black prints on my feet."

Sue folded the discarded newspaper and placed it back on the coffee table in easy reach for Hank in case he wanted to read it.

After taking Hank his beer, Sue hurried to finish dinner. Thick red sauce bubbled in an open pot on the stove. Fascinated, Sue watched as the bubbles popped, making a sucking, slurping "plop" noise then leaving splatters of red on the white stovetop. She automatically wiped away each splatter then stared at the pot again, waiting for the next "plop." Sue dipped a wooden spoon into the bubbling mixture for a small taste. She grimaced at the bland, acidic flavor of crushed tomatoes.

Standing on a chair, Sue searched the top cupboard above the stove for the small jar of whole bay leaves. It had been a long time since she made fresh spaghetti sauce or used any of her Italian seasonings. A small shaker of oregano fell onto the stove barely missing the pot of bubbling sauce. Next to it was a box of rat poison they'd kept after their last dealing with a nest of rats. A thought crept into her mind. Why not?

"Quit making so much noise, will ya?"

"I'm sorry, Hank. I'm making it just the way you like it." The End.

Soul Catcher

The last of the fading light disappeared into the glassy smooth surface. The stranger sat quietly on the beach watching the water swallow the blazing ball inch by excruciating inch.

This was just one of many beaches at sunset he'd seen and knew he'd see again. He anticipated the darkness. Savored it. Devoured it. He desired the blackness as it desired him.

In one fluid movement, the stranger stood as the last bit of light disappeared. He walked east away from the water. His steps light, barely displacing a grain of sand as he made his way to the spot he'd chosen earlier.

The stranger saw the chosen one only a moment before she was aware of his presence. Like the others, she searched frantically for a place to hide from his eyes while trying to appear in control. Nonchalant and unaware.

He smelled her fear – he needed her to fear. It made his actions easier; although it didn't appease his conscience; he'd have to have one first. Carefully taking his time, he set out his tools, fingering each one with loving attention.

###

Beads of sweat sprung on her forehead and the back of her neck. The tiny hairs that had escaped the topknot tickled the sensitive skin behind her ear, startling her. She stumbled, no longer in control. She fled to the only place she could find to hide, a tiny space -- her temporary safe haven. Small spaces comforted her. She sat, breathing fast and deep. Gulping at the precious air her body desired.

Then she heard it. Her sanctuary invaded. No longer safe. He was here. Trapped, she accepted that escape was impossible. She refused to go like a lamb to slaughter. She would not be sacrificed tonight. She would face him, this stranger, on her own terms. He wouldn't make her crack; she'd save her dignity at least.

###

The stranger would be patient. He knew from long experience that the means to the end would be the same. It was always better when he waited.
His only enemy for tonight's event would be dawn, but it was hours away. Still no hurry. The darkness would stay long enough.

Without looking directly at her, he watched as she stepped out of her safe cave, determined to show no fear. He smiled at her gumption. She was different than the rest. This could be a good thing. He fingered each of his instruments gently; knowing them by touch, not needing to see, only feel.

In the dim light, the stranger glanced at his prey. She took a deep breath. He knew it was to summon her courage knowing it was time to face him, the stranger who wanted her; needed her. Why he chose her she would never understand, only knowing he wanted her was enough to feed her fear.

He tossed her a piece of cloth; like the outfits they all wore; his choice, not theirs.

The tiny piece of fabric and string barely covered the gifts God gave them. It wasn't enough to hide their gifts from his unblinking eye. He would see – see deeper into her than anyone had ever tried before. She would give that gift to him. He would enjoy it immensely.

He would take what he needed, then leave seeking his next soul, his next thrill. No end in sight; no relief from his wicked muse.

Trembling fingers tied the final knot into the string that held the wisps of cloth to her body. She drew a shaking breath then stepped into his sight. He gave no notice of her appearance.

He sensed her fear and knew his indifference somehow might comfort her. He wasn't emotionally involved. Maybe tonight he would be quick. The process painless. No words. No noise; only silence.

He picked up his first instrument. He never knew which one he would use first until he saw her. Each girl was different, unique. But none were like her. She was perfect. He knew it the first moment he laid eyes on her. Tonight, he would capture her soul, and he alone would possess it.

Now his work began in earnest. He never spoke. He never did until he was finished. He motioned with his long slender hands, pointing with his thin fingers. She moved only at his command. It was best that way. He controlled her.

Flash! Snap. Flash. Flash! Click. Click. Snap. Flash! Her eyes blinked in the sudden darkness. It was over. Silence once again.

He commanded the silence; he demanded it. Only at his signal did the applause begin. That too was by his command. He came, he performed, he left. That was his way.

###

She stood, nervous, uncertain. Was it over? Did she survive? He signaled for her to leave. She made it back to the safety of the tiny dressing room.

She changed her clothes quickly, desperation fueling her moves. She didn't want him to change his mind. Not now.

###

He packed up his equipment with neat efficiency, tossing the small piece of cloth and string on top. It would never be used again. He moved quietly. Once again, he had hunted the elusive prey and once again, he captured it.

It was time to go.

Without a word, he left. No goodbye, no handshake. Only a small white envelope left on the table that once held his equipment.

###

She opened it carefully, fearing she'd damage the delicate paper.

Inside she found his card. And her check.

It would be weeks still before she knew if she made the cover. She could wait. She clutched the check to her chest. For now, this was enough. She'd made it. She was a swimsuit model.

The End

Ever Have One of Those Nights?

Have you ever noticed that awkward moment when you dig a hole to hide a body and find another body?

It happened to us tonight. We were going about our regular business.
Shovels, Pick ax, rug, body. We had it all down to a science, really. We even used GPS to determine where to dig. Because, like I said earlier, there is an awkward moment when you dig a hole and find another body.

Whose body was it?

Did we put it there and forget to log it on GPS?

Did some other company moving in on our turf?

All I know is we saw the body and all hell broke loose. Davey stepped on the shovel and fell over. Knuckles dropped the rug-wrapped body. I kinda froze; cigar chomped between my teeth; GPS in hand staring at the screen as if I were seeing it for the first time.

I gave the little handheld gadget a hard shake.

Nothing.

Was this an issue for the Boss? I didn't want to call him. Not this late at night.

Davey stood up, brushed off the dirt he'd accumulated from rolling around on the ground and peered into the hole. "Hey there really is a body in there."

I smacked him upside the head, "Of course there's a body in there, idiot! Do you think I'd make something like that up?"
Knuckles stepped over the body-wrapped in the rug and peered into the hole. He looked from the body in the hole to the body lying on the ground. "Hey, does anyone see a resemblance to the rug in the hole to this rug?"

I stopped messing with the GPS and looked. Knuckles was right. Not only was someone moving in on our territory, but they were using the same discount rug company we used.

I started to fume. This was our turf. We earned it. We worked hard for it. We did a good job. Our clients liked our work. This just wasn't going to happen, not if I could help it.

We carefully looked around, checking to see if anyone was watching. We squinted into the darkness, not seeing anything, as if we could see anyway.

Desperate, I gave the GPS one last hard shake. A blip appeared on the screen. The date and client name appeared in the information field. No wonder the rugs were familiar. It was one of ours.

I needed a drink. And a new set of batteries.

I half whispered-yelled, "Get to work, boys after this, we're celebrating."

"What for?"

"For not screwing up. For not having any competition. For not having to call the Boss." I gave them a crooked smile and pointed my half-smoked cigar at them, "and, because I said so."

"Good enough reason for me," Knuckles said as he lifted the shovel and began burying the body we discovered.

"Hey, where are we going to put this one?" Dave motioned to the rug- covered body on the ground.

I moved a few steps away, checked the GPS, and gave the guys a wave with my cigar. "Right here, boys. Right here."

"It's gonna be a long night." Davey dragged the body to the new dig site.

"Get back to work. I'm gonna log the new dig into the GPS. Remind me to stop at the convenience story on the way back to the shop to pick up batteries.

The End

The Storm

The day gave way to evening earlier than most.
There was no languid sunset with light slowly
fading away. The darkness enveloped the day,
like a black cloak. The wind, tentative at first,
grew stronger. It rustled the un-raked leaves in
the front yard blowing them about, some around
our yard, some into our neighbor's yard.

Deep rumblings resounded in the distance;
ominous threats of what were to come. Bright
zigzag flashes of light crisscrossed the black sky.
The gulf blackened; the water churned. My heart
pounded in my chest. I drew a shallow breath.
Panic settled in for a long stretch. I had no control.
Thunderstorms gave birth to instant anxiety
attacks.

I remember the first storm. The one that scared
me. I was a little girl, still young enough to
count my age on both hands. Thunderstorms in
the Spring were a sure sign Summer wasn't far
behind. Mommy and daddy gathered all of us
in the front room with our blankets and pillows
to watch the storm through the big picture
window. Bold lightning flashed and loud
crashes of thunder echoed between our
squeals of delight.

The lights flickered off then back on. Daddy looked at mommy. Mommy nodded and stood. Daddy told us to stay on the floor while he and mommy unplugged the TV and turned off lights. I stood. I was the oldest. I could help. Daddy understood and gave me my orders: Turn off the lights in the bedrooms and then unplug them. I could do it. Eager to show mommy and daddy that I was a big girl. I hurried to do my assigned tasks while my younger brothers and sisters sat and watched from their nest of blankets on the floor.

The first bedroom was easy. Only one light to turn off. Nothing to unplug. I felt so important as I went from bedroom to bedroom repeating the process.

My last stop was mommy and daddy's room. It was at the back of the house.

The rain and hail pounded the roof. Tree branches scratched at the aluminum siding and across the windows. I wasn't so brave now. I stood in the doorway to my parents' room. I couldn't make my feet move forward. Daddy yelled from the front of the house for me to hurry and get back out there. I took a deep breath, then took a tentative step into their bedroom.

BOOM!

CRASH!

WOOSH!

Blackness all around. Wind tore at my little dress.
My hair whipped around my face. I was wet. The
rain pelted my little body. I was scared.

"Daddy!" I cried. "Help!"

In mere seconds, I was lifted into the air by
strong arms. My daddy pressed me close to his
chest. I turned my face into his warm body
away from the cold, wet wind and rain.

I hated thunderstorms. Ever since that night, I
dreaded the gathering of dark clouds and
scattered lightning. I crawled into bed and held my
pillow tight. With shaking hands, I reached for my
anti-anxiety medication.

Eagerly, I swallowed the tiny pill. I laughed a
nervous, tight laugh. How could such a teeny, little
pill protect me from such a wild, intense force.

I waited for the pill to spread the familiar,
welcome calm over my body. I waited for the
storm to blow itself out. I waited for answers to
questions that had no answers. Why was I
living in the lightning capital of the world?

The End

My Dreams

My dreams are my own

Private, secure, alone

My dreams don't always appear

For everyone to see, that's okay

For me. Anyone else doesn't matter to me.

Dreams keep me moving forward, every changing, every evolving

Dreams keep me evolving, ever moving forward, and ever changing

Dreams keep me changing, ever evolving,

ever moving forward Dreams keep me.

No one can see my dreams but me, and that's

okay.

Sometimes life is all about risking everything for a

Dream no one can see, but me.

The End

Mother's Helper

I flinched. Congealed wax felt stiff and tight on the back of my hand. What had just happened? The faint odor of burnt candle and smoke filled the air. I wrinkled my nose in distaste. I looked down to find the dribbly, half-used white candlestick in my favorite brass holder hanging from my fingertips.

Its flame, long since extinguished. I dropped the candlestick holder and stepped back, nearly stumbling in my haste. I looked left, then right quickly. When had it gone dark? A faint buzzing in my ears wouldn't let me concentrate. I needed answers to fill the empty expanse in my mind that should have held memories of the last few hours.

Confused and disoriented, I shook my head, but the buzzing only grew louder.

A glare. There it was again. Oh, thank goodness. It was just the television.

Now, where was the remote control? What a silly question. Where else would it be? I shouldn't have to look far. It would either be in Dan's hand or right where he left it so he could go to the bathroom.

Dan!

Why was he sitting that way in his easy chair? How can he watch television from that angle? I took a hesitant step forward. My eyes strained in the darkness to look into his eyes. Vacant eyes.

"Dan?" I whispered.

No answer. No recognition. No breath.

"Dan!" I called out, louder this time as I stretched out my hand to touch his arm.

Thunk!

I jumped, frightened at the new sound. I shuffled my left food as something hard rolled across it. Keeping my eyes on Dan's ashen face, I knelt and ran my hand across the carpet. I strained further, not wanting to look away.

I stretched my fingers out and touched a round, hard shape.

I released the breath I had been holding. His damn hockey puck. He never watched a game without tossing that thing back and forth from one hand to the other throughout the entire game.

I sat down with a thump as my bottom connected with the floor. My mind crowded with disjointed images as I looked about the dark room.

Of their own volition, my eyes strayed back to Dan's. "Har-umph!" I chortled.
"Guess you won't be watching anymore hockey games when "Married …. With Children" is on."

I stood quickly, swaying slightly from the rush to my head. I steadied myself and then picked up my heavy brass candlestick holder. Mother said it would come in handy one day. She was right.

The End

Another Father's Day

The anxiety starts months earlier.
Expectations whittle away at my denial until I
can no longer ignore their penetrating
slashes. Piercing echoes rebound in my head;
the day is coming. The day is coming.

The cards lined up on the shelves in the store all
ridicule me. "Which one of us will you pick this
year?" they whisper tauntingly. I cringe at the
thought of perusing the sentiments inside each
small missive. What could I expect. These cards
are for happy occasions. Love and gratefulness.
To good fathers from thankful children. Who would
make a card for me?

I could forget to send a card. I think about that
rebellious act every year, but the guilt gnaws at
me until I give in and pick the least sentimental,
least personal card I can find, anxious to get the
task over and behind me.

It could be worse; the anxiety could turn into a
full-blown panic attack if I consider making a
phone call instead. I've thought about it each
time. But what would I say? What wouldn't I say?
The deafening silence. The unspoken
accusations. I didn't have the strength. A phone
call I didn't want to make. Memories I don't want
to remember. Missing memories I couldn't
remember. A father I didn't want to call my own

A past I longed to forget haunts me day and night. Why must I hide my pain? Why must I continue to act like all is well?

Shattered innocence.

A child's world no longer carefree. Where did that little girl go? Has she found peace? No, she's still here, hiding deep inside. Yearning for safe shelter. Where is my guardian, my strength, and my protection? Am I strong enough? Not nearly enough, but my power comes from within. I have the love of God and His protection. With that, I will protect the little girl. She has nothing to fear with me by her side. I'll hold her tight in the darkness, so she no longer has anything to dread. She can sleep safely while I stay awake and protect her from the shadow man.

Who was that man who insisted I call him daddy? That man who entered my life while I was too young to choose. Who was that man who made me afraid? Long nights awake in the dark too afraid to close my eyes too afraid to give in to sleep. Too afraid to wake up while the sun was still on the other side of the world. Daylight was my closest friend. Was my daddy like other daddies? Were all little girls afraid of the dark?

Shattered dreams and broken hearts, those were the crumpled discarded toys of my childhood. No happy memories of father/daughter moments; no ice cream, fishing, or special days. Only darkness, fear, and shame. Responsibilities too heavy for a child to bear hung around my neck like an anchor holding me in place.

I applaud that young, scared girl, who grew into the strong brave me. Who still fears the darkness and who still lives with the same. Yet, survived.

That man who is called, "Father" whose heart continued to beat within his chest; he lived on. How could a monster live? Each year he grew weaker, yet he lived on.

I survived as well. Each year I grew stronger, knowing the end would come someday. A heart would no long beat. When there would no longer be anymore Father's Days.

And now it is over.

The Shadow Man, daddy, Father, Monster, whoever you were; gone. And I am free. Am I bitter? No. Have I forgiven you? Yes. Have I forgotten? No.

However, I am ever so thankful that there are no more dreaded Father's Days for me.

The End

Found My Faith in the Past

I was a good, little Christian girl and went to Sunday School every week. Does that mean I'm going to heaven? Some people might think yes, because according to them I earned a "Get into Heaven Free" card for putting in my "time" by going to church. Others might say that every kid goes to church, and it only counts if you go to church when you're an adult.

All right, I'll indulge you because I too, might have bought into that idea. And, just to set the record straight, I went to church as an adult, too.

Do I still get to keep my "Get into Heaven Free" card?

No.

"Why?" you ask.

Because there is no such thing. It takes more than just going to church to get into Heaven.

"So," you ask, "what does get you into Heaven?" Or, more specifically, what does it take for you to believe that you will someday go to Heaven? God gives us the answer: Love Him and love others. Simple, right?

No doubt, but, to me, I add, "faith." That intangible ideal with such a broad range of definitions.

Faith isn't a certificate you get for going to church every Sunday. It doesn't get passed from mother to daughter, like the familial silver tea setting. Faith is something you have to learn-earn-over time.

It's easy to say, "I have faith" when life is wonderful, your car is running fine, and you have a paycheck that covers your monthly expenses.

It's even easier to say, "Just have faith" to others who are troubled.

But, what about during your troubled times? Do you have faith then? Do you hold onto your faith with both hands, using it to shield yourself against adversity?

Or do you curse God and the day you were born? Do you blame a hundred other circumstances that put you in that exact place at that exact moment to suffer so needlessly?

If this were a perfect world, suffering wouldn't exist. If this were a perfect world, we wouldn't doubt ourselves or our spiritual destination after death. But this isn't a perfect world, and faith isn't something you can pick up at the local market in case you might need it someday.

I truly believe that bad things happen to good people. I know this because I see it on the news. I know suffering, because I have suffered. Ordinary people suffer every day. Unfortunately, when emotions run high, we focus on each catastrophe, and faith gets lost.

What we fail to realize is that we earn faith through experience by knowing where to look and when to listen. That isn't always as simple as it seems, especially when you're dealing with a bad day at work, a rotten commute home, dirty dishes, and discontinued water service. It isn't always so easy to rely on just plain old "faith" then.

In the midst of a crisis, we usually turn to friends. They give advice like, "God never gives you more than He thinks you can handle." And, of course, the ever popular, "Things could be worse, you know."

So, where did God get the idea that I could handle so much and for so long? I wanted to know how much I could handle so I'd know when I was getting close to boiling over when things got worse. Did I know what I was going to do once I found my boiling point? No, of course not.

All through life, I thought the answers were "up there." All I had to do was pray to God. What did I get? Nothing. At least not the answers I thought I should have received. Like most A-type people, I assumed something was broken; something was wrong, and I could fix it. Maybe God wasn't getting my question in the right translation, or it was being misdirected.

Nothing was broken. The problem was me. I wasn't listening to what God was saying in return. One lonely night I finally heard.

As a writer, I feel very strongly about words and that's when I understood what I needed to do. I had the gift of sight and comprehension. I could read His words. I wasn't alone. I finally heard Him.

I turned to the story of Job. This was my answer. I heard Him. This time I had a better understanding of why God tests His people and their faith. I understand now why God could allow His people to suffer and still love them. He shows us His love by being there, at any moment, so we can ask for guidance and wisdom. He's very proud of us and loves us so much. All He asks in return is this: that we control our patience and have faith in Him.

His request isn't any different than our desperate prayers to Him in our darkest hour. How many of us have prayed to Him asking that He spare the life of a child hurt in an accident? Probably not as many who have prayed that we pass a test, get out of a speeding ticket, lose ten pounds, or get a particular job if only ___. You fill in the blank.

It was time. I started on a ten-year pilgrimage into my past. It wasn't easy. I didn't know what I was searching for or at that time it would take ten years to discover, but I knew I would find it. I needed to know how long I had been ignoring His signs. I succeeded. I found my faith and so much more.

At first, recalling my past was difficult. So many blocked events. I only saw small, broken fragments of my life. I used my photo albums to help me remember, but even then, it was an arduous task.

The worthy occasions of the past thirty years captured as single moments were frozen in time. The images faded now, from obsolete technology and forgotten events.

Growing up as a painfully shy, overweight, and acne-prone child, I kept to myself most of the time, always avoiding confrontations and existing on the outer edge of life. I faded into the background in life and in the sometimes-unfamiliar pictures.

Only the happy moments were captured in those big books. They could be my memories, if I wanted them to be. But it wasn't the real me. I wasn't happy. I needed to understand my past so that I could embrace my faith completely.

For a long time, I continued to search my memories until I found a tiny box in the far corner of my mind. I trembled as I opened it, fearing what it contained. The box was deceptively small. Its contents much bigger than its container. Another photo album, unlike the kind that you can hold in your hands and turn the pages.

More pictures, these were not faded by time or technology—vivid pictures depicting other events that occurred in my life. Images I can't show to my friends or my family. Only myself. No one would ever see or know what I was to never talk about: alcohol abuse, physical and mental abuse, and sexual abuse. I was frightened; horrified at the terrible incidences a child endured. Was it really me? I had to destroy these pictures.

I wanted to eliminate them as easily as setting a match to a piece of paper. I could see them burning in my mind. I'd put the match to the edge of the picture; watch the flame lick hungrily at the paper's edge. I would smile as the picture darkened; the edges curled in toward the heat. I'd hold the picture for as long as possible, watching the flame devour the scene, watching the moment go black. Then, like the charred paper, the image would flutter

away as ashes. Never to be remembered
again. If it could only be that easy.

I couldn't make the pictures burn and I couldn't
look at them anymore. I put
the box away. For five years, I piled other clutter
on top of that tiny box; pushing and shoving it
further in the back of my mind. Trying to forget.

It didn't help. Everywhere I went, no matter what
place I ended up in, somehow, when I least
expected it, I'd realize that box had found me.
Again.

I knew it was time. I gathered my strength and
once more reached in. I was astounded to find
that it wasn't so little anymore. And, it had
multiplied. Boxes of memories from failed
relationships, failed parenting tactics, and
debilitating illnesses. Boxes and boxes of
failures. Where were the good memories? My
eyes wandered to the piles of photo albums I
had accumulated.

I needed to change the way I was learning. I
examined each memory with God's eyes. I saw
something new. I wasn't alone during those
times. He was with me. He cared. He saw. He
knew.

It's been another five years. I've grown in spirit
since then and a wonderful thing happened to

my hiding spot. Other boxes have accumulated that contain good memories. Boxes now contained successful accomplishments, a remarkably supportive marriage, and happy memories with my children and my friends. Recollections of good parenting decisions and outstanding professional achievements tumble out each time I open a box. One box overflowed with the images of a dolphin racing through the water as I crossed the bay on a bright sunny morning. My faith has enabled me to fully experience every moment and take joy from every event, no matter how insignificant.

I still have that first little box. I don't often look inside; instead, I continue to add other boxes to the collection. In these boxes I've combined my memories. Some good, some not so good. All memorable. None hidden. All my memories together make up who I am. And who I am is the person God wants me to be. At least, I hope so.

I finally learned that I should have been always focusing on my faith in God, not just when I was in crisis mode. Instead of heading out in unknown directions to wander senselessly, I should have had faith to look for His signs.

Was it just coincidence that I've finally come to understand the true meaning of faith after nearly forty years?

I don't think so. I had to experience everything I did to become the person I am now. Although, being sensitive to detail, you'd think that I would have paid more attention. Instead, I blindly refused help.

I hear you asking me, "Would I still have willingly endured the pain and suffering to learn all that I have?"

Probably. Wait, the answer is a resounding yes, even if I had to feel every single painful moment again.

Pain is one of those emotions that help us focus our attention on God. Pain can get our attention real fast. It got mine; eventually. Unfortunately, I had a high threshold for pain and a memory blocking defense mechanism.

I was brought up in a world that used pain as punishment. My parents used pain-inducing techniques to gain our obedience. "Don't do that or I'll spank you."

Other people used pain to manipulate emotions. It was easy. How many times have we heard, "I love you so much it hurts." Or, "It pains me to tell you this, but . . ."

Pain makes us look inside ourselves whether we want to or not. However, pain shouldn't always be punitive. Sometimes, like in Job's case and in mine it can be used to instruct. I always thought I was an exceptional student. I've realized that learning lessons the "hard way" is still the best way to be taught. By turning myself over to God to teach me, I learned more than just how to have faith in Him. It was difficult to accept, but I learned so much.

My heart carried so much resentment and self-pity, that I couldn't see the good that I had in my life or the good in the real me. All of that has changed. I understand now that it isn't my job to make sure that all the evil of the world immediately be recognized and punished.

God created us with a free will. And, because of that free will, He wasn't going to intervene in our daily lives and administer instant justice. He wasn't going to raise His mighty hand and smite every person who did wrong. Not even if I stood waving with flags and flares to point Him to every single perpetrator.

I couldn't call upon Him to give the driver who just cut me off on the freeway a flat tire. And no matter how hard I begged; He wasn't going to strike my ex-husband with lightning for being a dimwitted knucklehead and not accepting the fact that I was right.

Again.

True justice required patience a lot. By gaining faith, I learned patience. Every time I drained my patience, I had to learn to wait for God to refill it. He would. I just needed to wait. He taught me patience.

Waiting for justice might seem unbearable, but God will mend those who have suffered without cause. He promised. Solomon said, "God will bring every deed into judgment, including every hidden thing, whether it is good or evil." (Eccl. 12:14)

Now I am content. I know that there was a reason I was born and a purpose for my being put here on earth. And, like Job, I no longer curse the day I was born. I ask Him to be with me as I travel from day to day and provide me with guidance and wisdom to know Him and make good choices.

I don't demand that He tell me why I had to go through what I did. His purpose is not necessary for me to know. I understand that there isn't always going to be a reason that makes sense to me. He knows the answers. And, maybe in time, I will discover them. Maybe. I trust God enough to understand that He knows, and I may never know.

That is enough for me.

And, in return, I promised God to listen more and complain less so that I can hear His gentle prompts. I am prepared to let go of what I can't control. So long as I have the opportunity to wake every morning and live one more day, I am content.

They, (you know who "they" are,) say that hindsight is 20/20. The signs were all there. I saw them. Strange how clearer they appear when looking backward.

You ask me, "Would I have done anything differently if I had known the outcome?"

No.

I know that I would have still marched to the brink of sanity and looked in wonder over the edge and beyond, leaping blindly into the unknown. If I hadn't, would I still be the same person I am today? Would any of these events have happened if I had the foresight to know the consequences of my actions?

All good questions.

I know what my answer is.

So, I'll ask you: "Would you?"

The End

Don't Tell Mother She's Always Right

My mother had an irritating way of always being right, no matter how many times I tried to prove her wrong. She told me that all I needed to do was stop trying and whatever I was looking for would find me. Sure, that worked great when I was looking for a job or my lost earring. But it's not what I would consider a perfect plan for finding love.

I'd had my fill of blind dates, double dates, first dates, and last dates. I didn't know if it was because I was getting pickier as I got older, but at thirty-two, I didn't want to settle.

And there was no way I'd stoop to answer the personal ads in the local newspaper. But doing my laundry on Saturday nights pretending I was getting a head start on the week was growing thin. There was no way I was going to call my mother and tell her I'd decided to take her advice. A month of denial had gone on long enough.

Instead, I waited another two weeks and told her in person when she invited me over for an early afternoon Saturday brunch.

"Are you going to eat that last strawberry, dear?"

"No, go ahead. I'm full." I leaned back in my chair patting my stomach.

"You don't eat enough, Savannah." My mother bit into the strawberry and wiped red juice from her lips with a pale apricot linen napkin.

"I'm the right weight for my height."

"Yes, if you were four feet tall."

I laughed. Mother did this every time we got together. "Mom, you're so funny." She detested the word "mom.", so before she could respond, I quickly changed the subject. "What about you? How's the bridge club?"

"The girls are the same. They're a bunch of old biddies that gossip more than a tree full of magpies. I don't know why I put up with them."

Mother pushed crumbs into a small pile, then into her hand. She carried them carefully to the trashcan. With feigned innocence she asked, "So, how's the love life? Still dating oh "what's-his-name?"

I sighed. Here it was. My chance to tell my mother I'm going to follow her suggestion. "I've stopped trying." I counted silently. One, two, three; a new record.

"Oh? You mean you've taken my advice?" She held a well-manicured hand to her beige silk-covered breast as if she were going to faint. Amazing how Mother always dressed to match the beige tones throughout the house. It was her decorator's idea of matching the sand at the beach – calm and soothing, he said. As if her mother would ever dare let one grain of sand cross her threshold.

"Yes, Mother." I poured the last of the orange juice into my glass and took a long sip before I continued. I smacked my lips in appreciation. Nothing like mom's fresh squeezed orange juice straight from her own trees.

"Oh, Savannah, ladies don't smack their lips together."

Making a great show of wiping my lips with the linen napkin, I lifted my pinkie high in the air, cleared my throat, and said, "Ah've come to the realization that Ah'm going to be happy with who Ah am."

Ignoring my theatrical dramatics, mother replied, "That's a good attitude, dear." She lifted her daughter's chin with a manicured hand. "Savannah, why couldn't you have put on some makeup before leaving your house?"

I scanned my mother's flawless, perfectly made-up face then stifled the sigh I knew was threatening to erupt. "Mother, it's 90 degrees outside and at least 110% humidity. Makeup just slides off my face. Go look in my car, it's probably all over my car seat right now. Oh, wait," I turned around checking behind me, "Here's some of it now." I wiped my hands on the back of my shorts. "Don't be vulgar, child."

"I'm not going to keep dating for the sake of dating. I don't need a man to make me happy. I have a great job. I own my own home. I even have my own retirement fund. If I'm destined to be alone for the rest of my life, then I'll darn well make sure that I do it in style!"

"Ladies don't say 'darn, ', dear." Mother cleared the rest of the dishes from the table and stacked them in the sink. "I've always said that if you stop looking that's when—"

"Mother," I interrupted her familiar lecture. "What's that pounding?" I heard a muted tapping coming from the back of the house. I had thought we were alone.

"Oh, it must be the contractor I hired." My mother brushed aside my question as if I'd just asked about the weather.

"A contractor?" I hurried through the immaculate living room. "Is the house in need of repairs?" I rushed to the window to look out. "Why didn't you call me?" I worried about my mother being alone since daddy died.

"Oh, stop worrying. You're such a fusspot."

I grinned at my mother's tenuous grasp of the modern language while I peeked out the window to check the activity outside. Strewn about my mother's Mexican tile patio floor, decorated with palm trees in large pots, were bits and pieces of board and screen. "Mother, did you check this person's references?"

"Yes, Savannah."

"Did you call the Better Business Bureau and see if there were any complaints filed against him?"

"Yes, dear, he's bonded and insured."

As I leaned further into the window, I wondered if she even knew what bonded and insured meant.
I saw a wooden stepladder that I knew didn't belong to my mother.

The jean-clad leg and utility boot balanced on the third step garnered my attention.

I jumped at the hand on my shoulder. "Like what you see?"

"What?"

"My new Florida room. Do you like it?" She swept her arm wide. "Of course, it's not much now, but it's going to be a wonderful addition."

"Oh." I pulled my eyes away before they traveled any higher up the leg. I shook my head to clear my senses. "Mother, you complain about too many rooms in this house now. Do you think adding another room is a good idea?"

"Don't you think it'll be beautiful?" Mother stepped further onto the patio and spread her arms wide already seeing her vision come to life.

"Yes. It looks like it's going to be great. What brought this on?"

"I've been meaning to enclose the lanai for some time now. You know how the mosquitoes get in the afternoon when the sun goes down. They practically feast on my poor skin when I try to enjoy the cooler evenings."

I tried to imagine a horde of mosquitoes feasting on my mother's perfectly groomed, twice weekly massaged skin. They wouldn't dare. "Well, I think it's great. When will it be finished?"

"Why don't we find out?" Before I could stop my mom, she had crossed over the piles of wood and screen to the legs I'd been admiring earlier. "Jake, get down from that ladder. I was just chatting with my daughter, Savannah." She motioned to me with a hand she held behind her back to come closer.

Subtle, mom; real subtle.

I dragged my feet across the thick carpet, eyes lowered; embarrassed by my mother's blatant matchmaking scheme. Out onto the patio I negotiated the piles with less grace than my mother. Catching my foot in an errant piece of screen, I fumbled to release my foot from its stubborn grasp.

She grabbed my hand and swung it between us. "Jake Lawson, this is my daughter, Savannah. Savannah Lake."

I grimaced as my mother emphasized the last name. "Hello, Jake. My friends call me Vanna."

"Vanna? Like Vanna White?" The man's face broke open into a dazzling grin. I couldn't help myself. I grinned back. It was only my mother's discreet cough that brought me back to my senses. "Uh, right. My mother says you're putting up a sunroom. That's wonderful."

Jake wiped his hands on his jeans. With my eyes lowered I caught every movement. His jeans were tight over his thighs; the material stretched across a solid mass. A flicker ignited in my stomach.

He held out a semi-clean hand. "Nice to meet you, Vanna." His voice deep, rich, and solid; just like the rest of him.

We shook hands; mine disappeared in his. A shock raced through my hand and up my arm. I jumped. Jake chuckled.

"Static in the carpet." I mumbled and rubbed the palms of my hands together to stave the tingling.

A perfect Cheshire grin graced my mother's face. I moved away to lean on the ladder, hoping to appear more poised. The ladder slid along the slick tile. Tools crashed to the floor. I flayed for a solid grasp. It ended up being Jake. Instead of crashing onto the ceramic tile I landed on Jake. My fingers curled into his crisp, white t-shirt as my feet went out from beneath me.

"Steady there." Jake said. I lay across his chest; arms and legs splayed in a tangled mess. I could feel his heartbeat beneath my hand. I spread my fingers open, palm down, on his chest. I lost myself in his eyes.

"I'm such a klutz."

"Here, you'll be fine." Jake helped me to my feet. "Sit." He led me to a wicker chair covered with a drop cloth. My mother pressed a glass of water into my hand. So much for appearing self-assured.

I turned to Jake. "I'm sorry, I'll replace anything I damaged."

Jake shrugged off my offer, giving his tools only a cursory glance. "It's fine. No harm done." He ran firm hands down my arms. "What about you? Are you all right?"

I squirmed under the attention and concern I saw in his piercing brown eyes. "Yes, I'm fine. Thank you." I cast begging eyes toward my mom. "Don't fuss over me." I caught a glimpse of Jake's concerned face.

"Right." Jake stood from his kneeling position in front of me all the while holding my eyes with a question. I answered without speaking.

He turned to my mom, "Mrs. Lake, would you mind if I knocked off a little early today?" Jake gave me a look filled with warmth. He had felt it too. The sizzling sensation that had started in my stomach flooded through my body. Tingles bumped up my arm, but it wasn't static shock this time.

"I don't see why not." My mother glanced from Jake to me. The look in her eyes told me I was going to hear from her later. "Do you have special plans?"

"I hope so." Jake looked down at me. "Savannah?"

I blushed under his warm stare. "We do."

Yes, it seems my mother was right. Again. Don't tell her I said so.

The End

Perspective

In the forest, there is a tree with a six-inch door.
Suddenly, the door opens and out bursts a tiny
purple fairy with glistening iridescent wings.
She wiggles and brushes shimmering dust from
her arms, then gives her head a shake. Her
ponytail trailing sparkling stars as she moved
her head.

"Who knocked on my door? "Tinkling melodies
filled the air.

"Uh, I think I did, but not on purpose," I replied. "I

accidentally fell against it." The melodious tone

returned. "No one has ever found the fairy

entrance."

My mouth formed a perfect "O." "I didn't even
know you existed." I motioned to the ethereal
sprite in front of me. "You're beautiful. Are you all
like this?"

"Yes!" More stars bounced around the fairy's
head as it bobbed. "I'm just a plain fairy. There
are others grander than me." The fairy tipped
her head sideways, looking at me. "Do you
have a name?"

"Yes, I'm Tina." Curious, I blurted, "do you have a name?"

"Yes, I am called Pansy." A twinkle blazed in her eye. "Would you like to meet the rest of the fairies?"

"But ..." Disappointedly, I looked down at her tiny body and gestured to the small fairy door. I was a small woman; however, I towered over Pansy. "I don't think I'll fit."

"Things are never as they seem in Fairyland." Pansy pulled her fist from a leather pouch and blew the dust toward me.

Delicate, shimmering flakes settled over me. My insides churned. Zip. Zip. Before I blinked, my world turned upside down. I opened my eyes and looked into Pansy's excited grin.

Sparkles of stars shot from her ponytail. I realized I was looking straight at her. We were the same height! I was fairy size!
A new adventure was about to begin.

The End

Skirting the View

The young lady lifted her skirt with her right hand while holding a paper bag of filled with groceries in her left. On tiptoe, she carefully stepped through the puddles forming in the parking lot.

Holding his briefcase over his head to dissuade most of the drizzle, he spied a bit of bare knee with the lift of her skirt. It normally wouldn't have distracted him as he hurried to cut through the parking lot on his way to work. He assumed it was the tentative way she stepped through the puddles as if at any moment one was going to engulf her. Her fragility awoke a sense of responsibility inside of him.

By stretching his stride, he reached her in a moment. That exact moment the damp bag of groceries lost their battle with gravity and the strain on the wet paper and collapsed out of her hand onto the pavement below.

"Good grief!" She stomped her feet, not noticing the splash of water over her shoes and onto his pants. Groceries tumbled about her feet. An orange rolled while the pint of milk made a splat and thud.

"Can I help?" the words flew out of his mouth before he thought.

Hands firmly planted on her hips she gave him a stare. "I don't know how, unless you can produce another bag." The light shining in her eyes erased the stern stare. "Can you?"

He laughed. Her sarcastic with the perfect antidote to the gloomy morning.

"I can't produce a bag, but here," he took off his overcoat and bent down to pick up the young lady's groceries. Cottage cheese, oranges, skim milk, bagels, and the list went on as he gathered the items into his coat and bundled it together, tying the arms for extra support.

"Here you go." He handed over the bundled coat to the young lady standing over him. Drops of rain dripping from her unencumbered hair and off the tip of her nose. He couldn't stop the grin from appearing on his face.

"I'm sorry I can't offer you my coat to keep the rain off, but –" he gestured to the bundled groceries held in her arms.

"I really appreciate it. You didn't have to go to all that trouble, just for me."

"Trust me. It was worth it."

She cocked her head and gave him a quizzical look.

"Let's just say I enjoyed the view."

"The view?"

He looked down at her legs.

Shifting the bundle in her arms, she lifted the hem of her skirt with a free hand. It crept an inch above her knee. A slow smile built on her face. A twinkle winked in her eye. "A tip for your trouble."

He gaped.

She dropped the hem of her skirt, turned, and walked away.

Picking up his forgotten briefcase, the rain no longer a bother, he whistled a popular tune as he ambled across the parking lot to work.

The End

Moments on the Beach at Sunset

My kite hangs motionless from my fingertips only moments ago soaring high, in the sky about the gulf. I stand now on the rough shell strewn sand of the water's edge, letting the small seaweed and sea foam thickened waves lap over my bare feet.

I watch the pelicans dive and swoop into the cresting waves at a prey only they can see and master. I'm amazed at their gracefulness for all their visible dizzy, spinning gawkiness. I watch the small terns as they hurry along the water's edge, attempting to catch the tiny crabs and other creatures from the water and sand. They're long legs remind me of branches of a tree.

I move to a large rock. A familiar rock. I've sat here before. I sit again. My journal rests in my lap. I'm not ready to open it yet to capture all my thoughts. I'm still content to soak in the images of the sun sinking into the gulf, the heavy orange ball falling into the darkness of the day as it grows bigger, and sky darkens to gray to purple to dusk. The people wandering; some with a purpose, others at leisure, while others still are only arriving for their nighttime fishing from the pier.

It's a glorious time on the beach as the sun sets over the water. A magical time that can only be captured with words or the perfect photograph that may or may not do it justice.

The End

My Griefs: Passing On

Disenfranchised grief is the pain of a significant loss that is not openly acknowledged or socially supported.

It's very hard to grieve for the losses that others don't understand or that possibly you yourself don't understand. Kenneth J. Doka, PhD, a professor of gerontology at the College of New Rochelle In New York, who created the term in 1985, said disenfranchised grief could be produced from any number of conditions.

I discovered a way to deal with disenfranchised grief and heal from it as well. I have suffered from many losses; and I found a gentle, safe way to pass on my griefs from my heart and soul to Mother Nature for safe caring. I'd like to share that process with you.

As I walked into the forest, I carried my griefs carefully, reverently, and with solitude.

What I was about to do takes ceremony and seriousness. These griefs had a hold in my mind and heart for a long time, a lifetime, for too many years; and it was time for them to go to their new home.

It was very natural to carry my griefs reverently to Mother Nature, to hold and contain for me what I'd been holding for nearly my entire life. My griefs included loss of innocence, virginity, and an unborn child; loss of giving life, loss of family, first marriage, and a trust in men; loss of mind to mental health; loss of back health to a car accident; loss of friends and an aunt, a mom; loss of half of life when I turned fifty; loss of grandma; loss of adolescence; and so much more.

I found my way to a spot where the earth was soft and pliable. I dug my hole and lay in it. When I lay down for my griefs to pass on, there was no wailing, no keening, and no moaning, just a kind of simple release. I let each grief seep from me into the earth. As each grief passed from my body to Earth's body, I felt a lightness, a release, a feeling or sense of closure that told me my grief had left my body and found safety in the arms of Mother Earth.

It took time. Some griefs had been with me a long time. They were reluctant to leave, but I was patient; and with gentle coaxing and loving reassurance, the grief passed on.

Finally, my vessel was empty. The process was long by not arduous, slow, and gentle—for my griefs and for me.

We had come to terms, my griefs and I. I have been their home for so many years; I kept them from harm. They in turn kept me from moving on at times.

So now they can rest easy in Mother Earth, knowing I'm still safe; but I will now be moving forward with grace, faith and perseverance. I'll always remember my griefs. But that's what they'll remain now—a memory.

The End

The Magic Miracle

Wakernesh stood over the small kettle hanging from the iron rod across the open flame. Heat combined with sumptuous odors rushed past his face escaping through the stone chimney above. He sniffed; his stomach growled in response.

"You old fool. Get away from that pot!"

Wakernesh shuffled himself around, careful not to trip on the ragged, singed rug in front of the fire. "Sephrina! Away with you, old hag." He waved his hand and flicked his arthritic wrist. His joints cracked as they attempted to obey their master.

Sephrina, pulling wooden bowls from a nearly empty cupboard, flinched.

A small spark jumped from the fire and sputtered onto the rug. It popped and snapped, breaking out into a small flame that threating to spread across the dusty, twisted rags on the floor.

Relief passed quickly over Sephrina's rheumy eyes. "Bah! Old man." She shuffled across the floor and stomped out the small flame. "Old, good for nothing, lousy broken down . . . " She mumbled under her breath as she carelessly ladled a portion of hot stew into a misshapen wooden bowl.

Wakernesh carefully lowered himself onto a rickety three-legged stool.
"Watch it old witch," he said with quiet even tones. "I've warned you."

"You don't scare me, Wakernesh." *Not anymore*, she added to herself. Slamming the bowl in front of him, spatters of hot stew speckled the front of his torn, threadbare tunic. "You are no longer the powerful wizard you once were." She dished more stew into another bowl and sat opposite her old husband. "We have been mortal now for over a hundred years, suffering dearly for it." She ran stiff, bony fingers through her lifeless white hair. Look at me! Not even a simple beauty illusion."

"Sephrina." Wakernesh covered her hand with his own liver-spotted, wrinkled one. "You'll always be beautiful to me."

"Bah! What do you know?" She threw off his hand and turned away, hot dry tears falling. "It would take a miracle to make me young again."

###

Late into the night, Wakernesh ruminated about Sephrina's claim. She longed to be beautiful again. A miracle she wanted. A miracle she would get. He worked through the hours of darkness pouring over dusty tomes, toiling over his mortar and pestle. As dawn broke, exhausted muscles aching, he was ready.

"Sephrina!" Wakernesh called with all the excitement he could muster.

"Now what, old man?" Sephrina stumbled out of their bed into their small living space.

"I've done it. I've created your miracle!"

"What are you babbling about, old fool?" Sephrina peered at him through the early morning light breaking through the small dirty window. "Have you lost your mind, too?"

"Not at all." Wakernesh carried a small vial to the table and sat down. "Here, look at this." He pushed the vial toward his wife.

"What is it?" She touched it with a tentative finger, uncertain of its power.

"Our youth, Sephrina! Our youth!" Wakernesh grabbed her hand with surprising strength. "Look at me, Sephrina." He pulled her toward him. "This is my last spell. Our last chance at youth. I've only enough for both of us to regenerate 150 years. I'm not as strong as I used to be. That's all I could do. We'll go back past the 100 years of being mortal and have fifty years as wizards before mortality once more."

Sephrina gasped.

"Think of it, Sephrina. We can be young again!"
Her eyes held his for a moment then slid greedily to the vial. "Are you sure it will work?"

"Yes, yes. Half for you, and half for me."
Wakernesh touched a tender finger to her wrinkled, paper-thin skin along a high cheekbone. "Are you ready?"

"My darling husband, you're exhausted. Why don't you take a nap, and we'll take the potion after you rest."

"You might be right. Maybe just a small nap."

###

Sephrina watched her husband shuffle to the small bed and sigh as he lay down. She touched the vial. Did it contain the powers her foolish husband said it did? She listened to his soft snores.

Without a second thought she uncorked the vial and swallowed the contents. "The old man didn't deserve immortality. He owed me for living in this squalor for a hundred years. I will be beautiful forever!"

###

Wakernesh awoke as the sun settled behind the hills. He felt a strange emptiness surround him. Tears sprang to his old eyes.

He found the empty vial on the table. "Sephrina?" He whispered. He searched under the table and behind the vegetable bin. He crawled on his knees to look under the bed. He peered behind the pile of wood next to the fireplace.

"Hissss-sstt!"

"Sephrina!" Overjoyed, the old wizard reached out to pull her toward him. He pulled his hand back and yelped with pain to find several straight thin red lines crossing the brown patches on his wrinkly hand.

"Now, now, Sephrina." He gently coaxed her out from behind the pile of wood. "Come here, little dear."

With her nose in the air, Sephrina left her hiding spot.

"That's a good girl." Wakernesh lifted Sephrina from her feet and sat her on his lap. He ran his hands over her thick, silky hair.

Sephrina stared at him with beautiful oval green eyes that seemed to wonder why he wasn't mad at her for taking the whole vial for herself. She tensed her body, preparing to bolt at the first sign of trouble.

"Oh, Sephrina. My darling." Wakernesh fumbled in his pocket and removed another vial of sparkling green liquid. "If you hadn't been so greedy, we would both be young wizards again."

Wide-eyed, Sephrina stared back, eyes on the small vial.

Wakernesh plucked the vial's cork and tipped it into his mouth. His eyes twinkled as he met hers. "Now, we'll just be wizard and wizard's familiar, my darling!" With a chuckle he swallowed the contents as the kitten in his lap yowled.

The End

The North Elevator

I quickened my pace, dragging my suitcase behind. Every third step it banged my heel, nearly causing me to trip. I refused to slow. The North elevator doors filled my view. Nothing else mattered, only making the next elevator car so I could get out of this airport.

There, the doors opened, I could make it, if I hurried. Damn, this suitcase. I stopped dragging it and picked it up, shaking it for a second as if it were an insolent child dragging its heels. I would not wait for another car.

The shiny doors began to close. I leapt toward them, pushing my arm through the narrowing space between them. The doors stopped, retracted, and then opened. Finally. I made it.

I pushed my suitcase ahead and tossed it to the floor as I fell against the cool wall to catch my breath. As I pushed number nine, I noticed number seven was already lit.

"Ow, excuse me," a soft, low, deep voice made its way through my foggy senses.

"Oh, sh--, uh, sorry for the suitcase, I really wanted to catch this ele— "then I looked up into the most awesome, clearest hazel eyes I had ever seen.

As he bent over to remove the suitcase from against his jean-clad shin, I looked down at his soft brown hair, peppered with an abundance of gray streaks. Just like I had always imagined.

In the next few seconds, my mind raced as my hands straightened, tucked, and smoothed blouse and hair. *What do I say? I threw my suitcase at him. My God, he must think I'm an idiot!*

With strong hands, he hefted my suitcase to its upright position and sat it gently next to me. My legs nearly buckled when he brushed his hand against my arm and asked, "okay?"

All I could do was nod with a silly grin plastered on my face.

He smiled back.

"You probably wanted to ride the elevator alone, huh?" I cringed as the words left my mouth before I could think.

He laughed. "Well, that was my first intention, but I think this is ok, too."

The elevator jolted to a halt as it reached the seventh floor. The doors slid open with a swoosh and a "bing."

"Good-bye, Mr. Ford." I called out, hoping I didn't sound too goofy.

He turned and put a handout to stop the doors from sliding closed. "Harrison," he said with a smile, then removed his hand. The doors closed and all I could see was my own smiling self, reflected in the chrome.

No one was ever going to believe this.

The End

Soaring Among the Clouds

Early morning rises; clear and bright.

A breeze shifts across the gulf –

I stake out my territory on the warm sand with a freestanding kite.

Just a small kite, a teddy bear-shape to claim my space on the beach.

The wind blows a pleasant scent of salt and seaweed

Into my face as I prepare my kite for flight.

I unfold the bright colors: pink, blue, yellow.

With a good gust up high it flies, twisting and turning.

I control it with my hands, looping and diving out over the water.

My kite is an extension of me – It flies; I fly.

Others walk by – stop and watch, I pay them no mind.

I'm in my own world – It's just my kite and me.

The wind blowing off the gulf; keeps us free.

Later, my arms stretched to exhaustion, I'll bring
the kite down to the ground,

Leaving the bear kite to stand sentry – I'll gather
my journal and pen, find a rock and write

About soaring among the clouds, my kite and me.

The End

Do You Believe?

If you desire to give your life a fresh start,
With God's blessing, I can help thee,
Ask the Lord Jesus into Your heart.
For I feel the Holy Spirit working within me

Do you believe Jesus came to Earth?
Son of God? Son of Man?
Mary's child of lowly birth?
To bring God's Word and thus began –

The chain of events from Judas' kiss.
Christ's crucifixion; buried in a tomb.
Christ's resurrection; the disciples' bliss.
Since Christ's ascension, they did resume –

Filled with the joy of the Holy Spirit,
To spread God's message of grace and love.
To tell us of all that we will inherit.
God's kingdom of riches in Heaven above.

Do you believe God is our Heavenly Father?
Do you believe Jesus Christ His only Son?
Do you believe in baptism by water?
Do you believe in the Holy Spirit are all in One?

So, now, repent your sins, confess to the Lord,
Commit your service, your heart to honor Christ.
Put on God's armor and take up your sword.
Grateful for eternal life; knowing Jesus' sacrifice.

God Has Always Been There

Dear Readers,

What was it about me and my connection to God? I knew Him enough to call on Him for protection and safety around the age of two when I was being beaten with a wire hanger and electric lamp cord by a babysitter. Who was it that brought my mother and father home at that exact moment and saw what was being done?

How did I know? All I can say is that I've always felt a presence with me that I knew was keeping me safe. And it was a place I could go deep inside myself to hide from the physical and emotional pain I endured by the men who beat me, sexually abused me and raped me. God made sure I was never truly hurt. Sure, I was left with night terrors, but oh my God, it could have been so much worse. I could have died! I could have been shot! I could have been sold to human traffickers. The horrendous situations are endless. I could have been left in the desert to die.

I think with God by my side, I ended up on the better side of life. And I'm here to tell you that God can do this for you, too. All you must do is have faith and believe. Really believe.

God is not some almighty presence that I call upon to invoke His powers when I've lost all hope and tried all other options. God is my first, last and only choice.

In 2022, my husband and I were flying our airplane and as we began our landing sequence, we lost engine power. Neither of us panicked. We were both calm and my husband flew the plane from the point of engine loss until we came to a stop in the orange grove we crashed into and slid through losing our landing gear, undercarriage, and parts of our wings. My only thought was, "God, You got this." Did I say it aloud? I don't know. I thought I did. I know I said it in my head. He was in total control.

When we completed the final crash stop, my husband notified the airport that we had crashed short of the runway. We survived and needed help. We exited the airplane as we could smell fuel and got far enough away while waiting for help to arrive. It wasn't very long. We were assessed at the scene by the Sheriff Department, taken to the hospital by the Fire Department Rescue Services and assessed in their emergency room. My husband had a couple of sore spots, but overall, he was uninjured. Thank you, God. I was immediately airlifted to a Trauma Center in at Tampa General Hospital for more serious injuries.

I was in shock for the most part. I couldn't tell you exactly what hurt, except my head. Other than that, I was in deep shock. At the trauma center, after tests, scans, and immediate care, I understood I had a brain bleed, concussion, and six broken ribs. I was kept there for two days and when released, I was still in shock. I still didn't feel any pain. I started feeling the broken ribs a couple days later and that lasted for over three months and then it took another three months to be completely cleared from my doctor's care.

The brain bleed and concussion recovery took about three months, as well. I didn't have any short-term issues with PTSD and flying. My husband started flying as soon as he could. For me it took a little longer. But we purchased another airplane, this time a larger one with more lounge seating in the back, so I didn't have to sit in the co-pilot seat. I was fine with that, if I took my anti-anxiety medication.

I flew in other airplanes and experimental airplanes. But, as time went on, the anti-anxiety medication stopped working and PTSD crashed hard over me. Now, I even have anxiety when my husband flies his airplane. I'm always worried that something is going to happen. He knows I worry. And I know he's a good pilot and can handle whatever situation he's put into. And I know that God is watching over him. However, with therapy I'm learning to find distractions to keep me from worrying and extra prayers for his safety fly on wings to God's ears.

As for me and flying, I don't think I'll get into a small airplane anymore. I believe I'm done with that. I have so many other health issues going on, I don't need to add unnecessary PTSD trauma if it's not needed. My husband and I don't own a traveling airplane anymore. So, that's not even an option for us. His airplane is for him to enjoy.

As for you, reader. I pray you never have to face any traumatic situation that puts you through dealing with PTSD or night terrors. May you have pleasant dreams and happy days.

"Truly He is my rock and my salvation; He is my fortress. I will not be shaken." – Psalm 62:6

I pray that God is your rock as well.

The Beginning

www.ingramcontent.com/pod-product-compliance
Lightning Source LLC
Chambersburg PA
CBHW060146130626
46556CB00006B/2517